WASHO
P9-CJP-500
3 1235 02876 2099

...ies

DATE DUE

"Say it will not happen, ... 'Say that Irrylath will not be killed."

The Ancient, her great, dusky hand so much larger than Aeriel's, brushed the tear from the pale girl's lips.

"I cannot promise you that," she said sadly. "Would that I could. But I have also seen him alive at the end of the war. You killed. You all killed. The possibilities are numberless, and no one is any more likely than another."

The Ancientlady eyed her very sadly now.

"Have you ever treasured something, child," she asked, "a thing so dear you thought you could never give it up—then learned you must?"

Cold terror returned to Aeriel. No. Never—not Irrylath! She shook her head.

Ravenna sighed. "Soon I must do so—give up what I love best for the good of the world. Come, child. Gird on your sword. The time has come for me to spell you the end of the rime and put my gift into the pearl. . . ."

RECEIVED

OCT 1 2 2002

NORTHWEST RENO LIBRARY
Reno, Nevada

The Pearl
of the Soul
of the World

The Darkangel Trilogy

The Darkangel

A Gathering
of Gargoyles

The Pearl
of the Soul
of the World

The Pearl of the Soul of the World

MEREDITH ANN PIERCE

Volume III of
The Darkangel Trilogy

MAGIC CARPET BOOKS
HARCOURT BRACE & COMPANY
San Diego New York London

Copyright © 1990 by Meredith Ann Pierce
All rights reserved. No part of this publication may be reproduced or
transmitted in any form or by any means, electronic or mechanical,
including photocopy, recording, or any information storage and
retrieval system, without permission in writing from the publisher.

Requests for permission to make copies of any part of the
work should be mailed to: Permissions Department,
Harcourt Brace & Company, 6277 Sea Harbor Drive,
Orlando, Florida 32887-6777.

First Magic Carpet Books edition 1999
First published by Joy Street Books and
Little, Brown and Company 1990

Magic Carpet Books is a registered trademark
of Harcourt Brace & Company.

Library of Congress Cataloging-in-Publication Data
Pierce, Meredith Ann.
The pearl of the soul of the world/by Meredith Ann Pierce—
p.   cm.—([The Darkangel trilogy; v. 3])
Sequel to: A gathering of gargoyles.
"Magic Carpet Books."
Summary: With the aid of a simmering pearl,
Aeriel battles the White Witch to free her husband Irrylath
and discovers her own true destiny.
ISBN 0-15-201800-X
[1. Fantasy.] I. Title. II. Series: Pierce, Meredith Ann.
Darkangel trilogy; v. 3.
PZ7.P61453Pe   1999
[Fic]—dc21   98-35707

Text set in Fournier
Designed by Kaelin Chappell

EFGHIJKLMN
Printed in the United States of America

In memory of M. M., who liked the first two

Contents

The Pearl
of the Soul
of the World

ONE

Pearllight

❧

SHE HAD NO IDEA WHERE SHE WAS—
only that she was in a cave, the walls pressing
close about her, all of white stone. Light came
from somewhere, dim and diffuse, and the air was
old: musty and bone-dry. She was thirsty, *so*
thirsty. All her limbs felt stiff, and behind her right
ear crouched a pain she knew she mustn't touch.
Her hair felt sticky, matted there. She gazed at the
featureless walls of the cave. She had been lost for
a long time.

Her stomach knotted, doubling her over. She
knelt on the hard, gritty surface of the tunnel floor
until the spasm passed. She must keep moving—
find food and water—or die. She had no idea how
she had come to be in the cave, only the certainty

that something was hunting her, following relentlessly: a Shadow, some living being, black as
night. She was glad of the light.

She managed to rise, and realized then where
the light came from. It came from *her*, from the
space between her breasts. Puzzled, she reached
into her gown to lift out what lay against her
breastbone, glimmering softly through the gauze-
thin fabric: a pearl, big as the end of her thumb.
It glowed with a faint blue light.

Memory teased her, only a glimpse, of a tiny
creature with lacelike wings, laying the pearl upon
her hand. How long ago had that been? She could
not remember. She put the pearl back into her
gown and, shining through the pale yellow cloth,
its light seemed white again. Frowning, the girl
examined the garment: yards and yards of air-thin
stuff. A wedding sari. Why was she wearing a
wedding sari?

An image formed itself unbidden in her mind:
a young man with dun-colored skin and long black
hair. His eyes were clear blue, almond shaped; one
cheek was scarred. What had he to do with her
gown? Dizziness overcame her, and she clutched
at the wall, sure that if she fell again, she would
be too weak to rise. She struggled to recall who
the young man was and what the pearl upon her

breast might be. But all her memories slipped away: beads hopelessly scattered from a broken string. The fierce ache in her head would not let her gather them.

A sheet of mirrorstone loomed before her, darker than the rest of the cave. She saw a figure in its smooth, polished surface: a tall, thin girl just crossing into womanhood, cheeks hollowed, fingers like bone. The pale, pale hair that fell to her shoulders was disheveled. Slant green eyes gazed blinking, huge as a bird's. She cast no shadow in the wan pearllight.

The girl halted, gasping, as the pang in her skull spiked almost unbearably. She must not see herself! The pain behind her ear forbade it, as it forbade her to know or to remember herself. She wrenched her gaze away from her own image and hurried past, for in that moment she realized just how lost she truly was: she had no idea *who* she was.

THE SOUND OF WATER CAME TO HER, A distant lapping plash. She stumbled into a run. The endless twisting corridor opened abruptly into a lighted chamber. A tiny stream cut through it, barely a hand-span wide in a bed thirty paces across. A mighty river had flowed here once, in ages past, reduced now to a mere trickle: its clear, clean brilliance played across the cavern's ceiling and walls.

The pale girl fell to her knees beside the stream and plunged her hand into its light. It was warm as lamp oil. She hadn't realized how she was shivering in the cool, dry air. Desperately, she licked the delicious drops from her fingers. Savory, full of minerals, the water tasted like crushed herbs. She knew there must be an easier way to drink, but she could not remember how. The trickling stream held her whole attention—so that she did not even notice the others standing in the chamber until the young one dropped his pick.

The sound rang sharp as a silver pin. The pale girl started up, water dripping from her forearms, and stared at the three people gazing curiously at her. They were very short, only a little over half as tall as she, and were dressed in trousers and sarks with many pockets. The two men wore caps. Their leader seemed to be the woman, whose fair, silver-coppery hair fell in four thick braids, one before, one behind each ear. She stood upstream, hands on her hips. The younger of her companions hastily caught up his pick.

"Reckon it's dangerous, Maruha?" the boy asked.

The woman shook her head. "Can't say, Brandl. An upperlander-from-under-the-sky, by the look, if I remember my learning."

She cocked her head and studied the girl. The upperlander stared back, wide-eyed, afraid to move. The squat little woman's eyes were the color of dark grey stones.

"But what's it doing so far underground?" the young one, Brandl, asked.

"Witch's work," the older man murmured, stroking his beard. "Could be the Witch's work."

"Bite your tongue, Collum, you fool." Maruha turned on him. "None of *hers* could ever get down here. We've wards."

"That one got through," the bearded one answered. "Perhaps only the first of many. We've known for a long time the end must come."

"Enough," hissed Maruha with a glance at Brandl. "You'll frighten the boy."

The pale girl watched them, her heart banging painfully against her ribs. She had seen such a creature once before. A little man with stone-grey eyes. The fragment of memory needled her, merciless, then vanished. The woman took a step toward her.

"You, upperlander, who are you?" she called.

The other flinched. She wanted to answer, but

her throat tightened till she could hardly breathe. "Uh, uhn . . . ," she managed, choking. A thin wail threaded past her lips. Her head pounded. She stopped, whimpering.

"Can't speak," bearded Collum breathed. "Witch's work."

"Look how thin," Brandl said, bolder now. He pointed, taking a step closer to Maruha. "Cheeks all sunken in."

Collum snorted. "All the upperlanders look that way: spindly as spiders."

"Nonsense!" Maruha exclaimed. "She's done in. Look at her hair and the dirt on her face." She came a few paces closer. "Girl, can you understand me?"

The upperlander tensed, ready to run—but she didn't want to leave the water. A kind of shriek issued from her lips. She understood, but she could not answer.

"Aye, but look at her robe," Brandl whispered, fear sharpening his voice suddenly. "Fine yellow stuff and not a rip or a smudge. It *shines*, almost. Like ghostcloth."

His companions started, and the three of them drew back. The pale girl's knees gave. She sank down, unable to go another step. Collum gripped his pick and pushed past Maruha and Brandl.

"She's the Witch's work, I tell you, and the sooner done with the better."

"No!" Maruha cried, catching Collum's arm. "She was drinking from the stream. None that serve the Witch can abide clean water's touch—"

Collum hesitated, lowering his arm. He glanced at Maruha.

"Marvels, I grant you, as yet unexplained—and her coming here may indeed be Witch's work," Maruha insisted. "But I do not believe that *she* is Witch's work, or that she means us any harm."

The girl sat in the sand, not looking at them. She no longer had the strength to lift her head. She heard Brandl edging closer to the other two.

"There's blood in her hair," he whispered. "Look."

"You see?" snapped Maruha, giving Collum a shake. "That is why she cannot speak." She took his pick from him roughly and thrust it into her own belt. Turning from him, she softened her voice. "Here, girl. You're hurt." Moving closer, she continued, "We are duaroughs, child. Let us help you."

The pale girl felt the little woman parting the hair just behind her ear and started. She batted at the square, nubby hands feebly, once. Gently, the duarough's touch returned.

"You needn't fear us. Sooth! What's this? Collum, Brandl, look. There's something here, behind her ear—jabbed in through the very bone."

All three crowded around her then. She did not look up. She gazed at the sand, at the warm, fragrant water lying beyond her reach now. She longed for it.

"Sweet Ravenna!" the young one, Brandl, exclaimed. "It's a silver pin."

"All mucked with blood." That was Maruha.

"Witchery," muttered Collum.

"I can't quite...," Maruha began.

The girl felt a shooting pain behind her ear and screamed. With a gasp, the duarough woman jerked her hand away as the upperlander pitched to the sand, covering her head with her arms, shrieking. They mustn't touch it! No one must touch it. She herself must never so much as lay a finger on the beautiful and terrible silver pin. Maruha sat down upon the sand, cradling her hand.

"Lons and Ancientlady!" she panted, flexing her fingers and then shaking her hand. "But that thing *is* Witch's work, and no mistake. It's *cold*, colder than shadow."

"It hasn't harmed you?" Brandl said anxiously.

"No, I only brushed it—lucky! Sooth, we must

take this child back to the others when we finish our circuit—"

"Fie, no!" Collum protested. "If she's Witched, she mustn't come within leagues of our last hidden hold ... !"

"Oh, be still," Maruha growled, getting to her feet and dusting the sand from her. "The child is starving and thirsting and in need of our help."

Help. The word reminded the pale girl of something, something. ... She remembered the face of the young man again, lit only by starlight, half-turned from her. "You cannot help me," he whispered. "I can love no mortal woman while the White Witch lives." *Help, help me!* she wanted to cry, but the pin robbed her of speech as well as of memory. The young man's image faded even as she groped for it. She buried her face in her arms and wept. Maruha bent to touch her.

"Come, child," she said softly. "Come with us."

The girl lay unmoving, spent. Nothing made sense. She was so weary. She wanted only to rest. Maruha took her by the arm and hauled her up-right.

"Help me, Collum," she panted. "We'll have to carry her."

The bearded duarough remained where he was, arms folded. It was Brandl who came and took the upperlander's other arm. He smelled of grease and candle wax. The scent made her stomach twist and clench, she was so famished. She felt she might swoon. Maruha glared at Collum.

"Suit yourself," she snapped. "I do not know who this child is or why she wears the Witch's pin. But I do know that it marks her as no friend to our great enemy, and by the Ancientlady Ravenna, I mean to get it out."

TWO

Underpaths

～

FISH, DELICIOUS FISH, EACH AS BIG AS
her finger: grilled in oil with succulent white flesh
and bones as soft as sprouting shoots. The pale
girl licked her lips and searched the dish for more.
She had been without the duaroughs how long now
—a week of hours? A daymonth? Here belowground, without the light of Solstar and the
infinitesimal turning of the stars, she had no sense
of the passage of time.

Her companions spent hours tramping the endless corridors, laying camp only at long intervals.
The pearl's faint glow passed unnoticed in the
darting glare of the fingerlamps the duaroughs carried. Brandl's gaze was always on her; he looked
away. Maruha was the kind one, giving her food

and drink, even combing out her matted hair, careful now to leave the silver pin alone. The pale girl shivered at the thought of the pin. It never ceased to pain her, but she found that as long as she did not try to remember or speak, the ache was bearable.

She and the duaroughs passed no more open water on their treks, though they crossed many more streambeds—all dry. The underpaths were desiccated, their moisture long vanished. Yet, Maruha always knew where to find water at need. From time to time, with one well-placed blow of her pick, she could release from the passage wall a thin spout. Then the girl drank greedily until Collum shouldered her aside so that he might fill their waterskins. After, Maruha stopped the flow with a peg and marked the wall with a complicated scratch. They moved on.

Whenever they came to a fork, the duaroughs paused and consulted a square of parchment: ancient, brown, and cracking along the folds. The girl saw lines crisscrossing the surface, some of them leading to a great starburst in the center. None of it meant a thing to her. She could not read.

Now and again, they came upon Ancient machinery, and each time, the duaroughs halted to examine it. Long untended, crusted with green and blood-colored flakes, most of it hardly functioned, only the faintest hum coming from its clockwork depths. Some of it did not function at all. Maruha shook her head once sadly when Collum rushed to press his ear to a device.

"We could save it," he said softly. "It wouldn't take long. Only half a hundred hours—we could save it! It hasn't been tended in years upon years."

Maruha again shook her head, more firmly now. "We're just a survey expedition. Mark it on the map, and others will come to tend it in our stead."

"If it lasts so long," Brandl murmured.

Collum rose, scowling furiously, and stalked away.

"Perish the Witch," the pale girl heard him mutter. From beneath tangled brows, he glared at her. "Perish the Witch and all her works!"

More often than not, the paths they took were narrow and precipitous. Maruha usually went first, her fingerlamp bobbing. Brandl followed, shepherding the girl, with Collum bringing up the rear. They had taken one such way not many hours past: bits of the ceiling littered the steep grade, which seemed not to have been traveled in an age.

"Fine path this is," snorted the bearded duarough, losing his balance and sending a shower of scree down upon the others. "If such were all they had in Ancient days, it's a wonder any of them survived to reach the City." The last word was mumbled, his voice taking on a superstitious edge.

"I've told you, this isn't the main path," Maruha snapped, her fingerlamp waving wildly as she scrabbled to keep her own footing. "It's back alleys and service corridors we're taking. The pilgrims' roads were sealed long since. You know that."

"When Ravenna first withdrew from the world?" Brandl ventured.

No one answered him. Gingerly, he guided the pale girl over the rough, slippery stones. She never lost her footing, moved with an unerring sureness, listening without attention to what the others were saying. The pain of the pin lessened when she did not concentrate.

"Do you think we could ever go there?" the young duarough tried again. "To the City? Just to see it. We're so *close*."

"No!" Maruha threw back over one shoulder. The path was too precarious to let her turn safely to glower at him. "It's sealed. No one's been to the City of Crystalglass in time out of mind."

A little silence. The pin stirred. Deliberately unfocusing her thoughts, the girl watched the play of lamplight on the walls for a few moments until the twinging ceased. Behind her, Collum slipped again and cursed.

"Oh, stop complaining," Maruha panted. "Taking these routes, we're less likely to meet weaselhounds, or others of the Witch's brood."

Beside the pale girl, Brandl shuddered, but no one said anything more.

They had laid camp not long after, and the duaroughs now sat at their ease. The girl licked her fingers again. There were no more fish. Her eyelids slid sleepily halfway down. Surrounded by companions, she felt safe from the Shadow's pursuit. No memories had troubled her during their last march. The pin hardly hurt at all now. She sighed lazily, scarcely heeding what the other three were saying.

"Well, tell me the use of keeping her," Collum was muttering, combing his fingers through his coarse grey beard. "Our people have no craft for the removing of such a pin. We are skilled in the maintenance of Ancient devices, not in instruments of witchery."

Beside him, Maruha sighed. "If only my brother were here! He would know what to do.

Sorcery was always his study, never machines."

"Your brother vanished into the upperlands handfuls upon hundreds of years ago," the other answered. "Fine help he is to us now."

Their talk subsided. The duaroughs had been gaming earlier with counters of stone upon a painted board. Now, their diversion done, the board lay to one side. The girl played with one of the small round stones. Like a bead it was. If only she had a bore, she could make a hole in it and put it on a string. The quiet rumble of the duaroughs' talk was comforting to her, even as she refused to follow what they said.

"Perhaps we should take her back to the upperlanders," Brandl suggested. "They have sorcerers. Let them heal her."

"Aye, that's exactly what the Witch would want us to do," grunted Collum, "show ourselves aboveground—" His voice grew vehement. "So that she can steal us away as she has done all our fellows...!"

"Peace, Collum," the duarough woman said. "We have all lost kith to the Witch. But we must not dwell on it—we must go on running the machinery of the world as best we can until the Ancient Ravenna returns to us. It is all we can do."

The upperlander tossed the beadlike stone in a circle before her, passing it from hand to hand. Other stones from the gameboard joined it, seemingly of themselves. Someone had taught her to toss stones so once, to pass the time—a blue-skinned girl in Bern? Memory teased, then darted away. Quickly, the pale girl willed her mind to emptiness. She tossed the stones without thinking.

His back to her, Collum murmured bitterly, "If the Ancientlady were ever to return to us, she would have done so by now. We are lost, and the world is lost."

"Courage, fool," exclaimed Maruha.

"The Ravenna is dead," the old man said.

With a look of alarm, Brandl whispered, "She can't be. If she is dead, then nothing matters...!" before Maruha shushed him.

"Give in to despair, and you give in to the Witch," she said to Collum.

Absently, the girl made a figure eight of the stone beads in the air before her and gazed beyond them into the fire, a warm dance of flame shooting upward from a metal vessel unlike any lamp she recognized. Folding his arms and turning away from Maruha, Collum caught sight of her.

"Now what's she doing?" he cried.

"It's more of that tossing—what do you call it?—juggling," Brandl said. "She always does that."

Stringing beadstones through empty space, she felt the heat of the fire traveling over her skin. She had felt such heat once before—though far hotter—from a far greater and stranger Flame, which had lit the pearl and had taken her shadow away. Uneasily, she banished the thought.

"Make her stop." The bearded duarough shifted nervously. "It's witchery."

"It isn't," Maruha said. "Leave her alone."

Abruptly, the girl let the beads fall in a heap beside the board. Even that mindless activity sparked memories which the pin forbade. Pain bit at her skull. Wincing, she shut her eyes and waited for it to subside. She was so weary of the ache. If only she might sit here forever, warm and well fed, thinking of nothing—fearing, dreaming, anticipating nothing. Silence.

"Time I was off." Maruha stirred. She caught up the two waterskins that were empty and started away, calling over one shoulder, "Keep watch—and look after the girl."

COLLUM GRUNTED. THE PALE GIRL BASKED in the warmth of the flame. The sound of Maruha's steps vanished down the corridor. Presently, the girl opened her eyes again. Collum had put up the beads and board and pulled the faded square of parchment from his pocket. Brandl opened his pack and drew out a tiny, slender harp made of silver wood with golden wires. The girl had never seen it before. He began tinkering with the tuning pegs and polishing it carefully with a fawnskin cloth.

"Best not let Maruha see you at that foolishness," Collum murmured. Brandl hunched protectively over the little instrument. At last he tucked the cloth away.

"Collum," he said.

The other made a wordless sound. The young duarough seemed to take it for encouragement.

"Tell me what you've heard," he said, with a glance surfaceward. "From up there. About the war."

Rattling his parchment, Collum turned away. "I wouldn't know anything of the sort."

Brandl bent closer. "You do! You're always listening. And I know you talk to the others, the ones who go surfaceward. You needn't fear to tell me. Maruha will never know."

The older duarough snorted and said nothing. The upperlander watched them, absently.

"I know I'm young," Brandl said. "But war doesn't frighten me. It's the *not knowing* that does. There's a song they're singing now, about a sorceress aboveground who's gathered an army to fight the Witch."

Collum started and turned. "If you know that, then *you've* been listening."

"I have." Brandl caught the older duarough's arm. "But you could tell me more."

Collum glanced in the direction Maruha had gone. He shifted uneasily. "Oh, very well," he sighed. "I'll tell you what I know, young one— but only so long as not a word goes beyond you."

The young duarough nodded eagerly. Collum set down his parchment. The pale girl saw him glance once at her, but she kept her mind and features blank. Whatever the duaroughs were saying, she told herself it did not matter.

"Now hark," Collum began. "You know how, many ages past, this world was a dead and lifeless one—until the coming of the Ancients from Oceanus. The Ancients changed this world and kindled it to life, planted herbs and grasses, fashioned peoples and living creatures. They made the tall upperlanders for the surface above, and us to run the world's engines below."

He glanced again toward the girl at the mention of her kith, then back to Brandl.

"You know all that, boy?"

"Yes, yes," the young duarough said. "Maruha saw to my learning."

Collum humphed. "And you know that the Ancients ruled wisely and well for uncounted years, until suddenly, unexpectedly, Oceanus called them home. Most departed at once in their fiery chariots, never to return. But a handful stayed behind, unwilling to abandon us. Yet even those withdrew into the desert, sealing themselves away in their great domed Cities. Only the Ravenna's remained open, and people made pilgrimages to her City of Crystalglass."

The younger duarough nodded; Collum continued.

"The Ancientlady instructed our folk in the service of those devices that manufacture the world's water and air, and she created the lons— great guardian-beasts—to shepherd the upperlanders above. But even she in all her wisdom could not keep the world from beginning to wind down: atmosphere bleeding off into the Void, weathermakers falling slowly into disrepair."

Brandl's breath quickened. "There's a word for it," he whispered. "An Ancient word: *entropy*."

Collum glowered at him to be still.

"Ravenna saw but one hope against our declining world's eventual collapse," he said, "against this *entropy*. Since Oceanus remained deaf to her entreaties, her fellows there refusing to lend their aid across the Void, she realized that she must conjure the means to rescue us herself. Thus she withdrew into her City a dozen thousand day-months past to begin the weaving of a mighty spell that would halt the entropy and restore the world."

Collum toyed with the folded parchment and at last put it away.

"All of this you know, Brandl."

The young duarough snorted impatiently. "Yes!"

His companion cast another furtive glance over one shoulder as if to be sure Maruha were truly gone. Brandl leaned forward intently. As the pale girl watched them, she tried not to listen, struggling to retain the blank emptiness of her mind—lest the pin take revenge.

"After the Ravenna withdrew, we strove to live as best we could without the Ancients' guidance. Then the Witch appeared. None know who she is or whence she came, save that she is a water demon, a lorelei. She dwells beyond the desert's edge, in parched regions known as the Waste. Beneath the dark surface of a still, silent lake, her palace stands, cold as poison and fashioned of transparent stone.

"She has, through her sorceries, beleaguered the whole world with drought. Even the once mighty wellsprings of Aiderlan have ceased to flow. Her weaselhounds sniff us out belowground. Who knows what fate awaits those they seize? And she harries the upperlanders as well, stealing their young boys over the years, half a dozen of them. These she has made into darkangels—the icari—each icarus a soulless demon with a dozen dark wings blacker than shadow. Her icari in turn conquered the six strongest nations of Westernesse, transforming the guardian lons of those lands into gargoyles.

"Then the Witch stole a seventh 'son,' a prince of Avaric, Irrylath, gilding his heart with lead and making him into the beginning of a darkangel. As soon as her spell upon him could become complete, she knew she would have half the world in her grasp. In terror, the peoples of Westernesse cried out for the Ravenna to return and vanquish the Witch. But Ravenna has not returned. Her City remains sealed. None know her fate."

Collum choked, his words growing harsh.

"Some fear her dead."

Brandl tried to catch the other's eye, but the bearded duarough would not look at him. The pale girl shrugged nervously, drawn into the tale despite herself. She knew she should not listen— and yet a kind of hunger filled her, a longing for news, for word of the world above. She found herself harkening without meaning to, and the pin twinged warningly as the duaroughs resumed their talk.

"No, it is not the Ravenna who has come forth to oppose the Witch, but another, the dread sorceress Aeriel. Some say she is the Ravenna reborn; some say she is her heir. But whoever she may be, she has, by means of her great magic, freed both Prince Irrylath and the Ions from the Witch's enchantment. The Ions are no longer gargoyles, Prince Irrylath no longer a darkangel."

Collum laughed suddenly, as though hope were beginning to return to him as he warmed to his tale. Wincing, the pale girl shuddered.

"Irrylath loathes his former mistress now and has raised a great army to Aeriel's cause. He has sworn to plunge his sword Adamantine into the Witch's heart with his own hand, for love of the sorceress Aeriel."

Brandl sighed, gazing up at the close stone ceiling above the white flame of their little fire. "Yes, that. *That* is what I long to hear of. If only I could be with them," he murmured, "up there, where things *matter!*"

The upperlander shifted fitfully. A desperate restlessness seized her. The pain in her head throbbed. She sat hunched, trying to block out the sound of the others' talk.

Collum grunted disapprovingly at Brandl's words. "Hold now, boy. Our life is here, along the underpaths—unless you want to run off like Maruha's worthless brother. There are few enough of us left as it is! The gears of the world won't go on turning of themselves."

"But on this war hangs the very fate of the world!" the younger duarough protested. "And it's the Witch's doing that our numbers are now so few...."

"All the more reason we should tend to our work." Once more, Collum cast his eye uneasily down the corridor Maruha had taken. "Where *is* she, I wonder?" he muttered. "She has been gone a rare long time."

Brandl paid no attention. He had lifted the little harp from his knees, strumming his fingers across it absently, and begun to sing.

> *"On Avaric's white plain,*
> > *where an icarus now wings*
> *To steeps of Terrain*
> > *from Tour-of-the-Kings,*
>
> *And damozels twice-seven*
> > *his brides have all become:*
> *A far cry from heaven,*
> > *a long road from home—"*

The pale girl listened in horror to the rime. Its music stirred her disjointed memory as words alone had not. The pin twitched, pricking her. Images swirled unbidden through her mind, stringing themselves together like beads of fire: the kingdom of Avaric ruled over by a darkangel, who stole young girls to be his brides. A darkangel become a mortal man again, astride a wingèd steed, raising an army to fight the Witch....

The girl gasped and trembled as the pin shivered, biting down. No force of will could stop the incomprehensible glimpses now juggling through her mind. Oblivious, Brandl in his clear, sweet voice sang on. Those words! She could not bear the tangled, shifting memories they brought. Every line of the rime caused unspeakable torment. The pin twisted, and another jab of pain went through the pale girl's head. A shriek of agony tore from her throat.

Springing to her feet, she plunged at the source of the music. Brandl looked up in astonishment as she snatched the harp from his hand. She flung it away, flailing at the young duarough. With a cry of surprise, Brandl fended her off. Collum jumped to his feet and seized her arms, pulling her away. She kicked and struggled, her bare feet shoving up sand. She felt hot metal underfoot for a moment, and then the fire went out.

"Blast!" exclaimed Collum. "She's overturned the lamp."

The girl scrambled free, one hand going to her breast, covering the pearl, hiding its light. In the pitch dark, she could see nothing, but neither could the other two. She heard them blundering about.

"Quick, boy, get it up before the oil runs out." That was Collum's harried voice.

"I'm trying!" Brandl's. "There, I've got it. Get your tinderbox."

The pale girl retreated, stumbling blindly down the jet-black corridor. Shadow: shadow everywhere! She was wrapped in shadow, surrounded, smothered by it. She could not breathe to scream.

The sound of rummaging, of flint striking metal. A spark in the darkness behind her, then a second spark, a finger of flame. She ducked into an open tunnel's mouth. A little light strayed after her.

"What came over her, do you think?" That was Brandl, his voice already faint with distance and the distortion of the caves. "She was never wild before."

"Your blasted harp music," Collum growled. "That set her off."

"No. She was restless before, kept looking at us, like she wanted to speak."

"Nonsense!"

"*You* wouldn't have noticed."

Panicked, the girl turned and fled, hiding her light. She wanted only silence, blessed silence, free from pain and memories. The pin behind her ear nestled deeper, stabbing her mind. She started to whimper, and then bit off the sound, afraid of being heard. Their voices were the barest ghosts now, hardly audible above the whisper of her running feet.

"Trim the wick, boy. No need to waste oil—"

"Collum, where is she?"

"What?"

"*Collum.* She's gone!"

THREE

Weaselhounds

SHE LAY IN DARKNESS, CURLED AROUND the light of the pearl. If she stayed very still, then perhaps the horrible, tangled string of senseless images evoked by Brandl's song would not return. The pin behind her ear throbbed still, though the worst of its pain had passed. She was afraid of the Shadow, here in the dark, but the terrible rime frightened her even more. Exhausted, she dozed.

A scuffing sound brought her sharp awake. How long she had slept, she had no way to tell. Her legs were cramped to numbness, her stomach tight, mouth dry. She was shivering so hard her jaw ached. Something moved beyond the bend in the narrow tunnel. Terror seized her for a moment as she realized it must be the Shadow. Then

Maruha came around the curve of the tunnel, a fingerlamp flickering upon one hand.

"There you are!" the duarough exclaimed. "I had nearly despaired of ever finding you, you strange girl."

The pale girl stared at her, tensed and frightened still. She laid one hand over the pearl, hiding its light. Maruha drew closer, carefully, as though afraid of startling her.

"Collum and Brandl swore they'd no notion why you ran off, but I got it out of them in the end."

The duarough laid her hand gently on the pale girl's arm, and when the upperlander did not bolt, she seemed glad. With a puff, she sat, obviously weary.

"That fool Brandl and his barding. He should know better than to sing of the Sorceress War in front of you."

The girl felt a breath of reassurance pass through her. Maruha would not recite the horrible rime that made the pin ache so. She felt safe now that Maruha had found her.

"And with the Witch's pin in your head, you doubtless know more of that grim conflict than we. How much of what we say do you understand, girl?" The little woman eyed her closely. The up-

perlander shifted uncomfortably, looked away. She
did not want to understand, dared not. In a moment, Maruha shrugged. "No use asking, I suppose. If only you could talk!"

She patted the pale girl's arm.

"Here, child, are you hungry?" She fished in
one of her many pockets and drew out a square
cake that smelled of honey and pungent dram.
"It's been ten hours since you ran away."

She broke the cake and held up one half to the
girl, who snatched it from her. The dense stuff
tasted sweet and tart, but her mouth was so dry
she could scarcely swallow. Maruha's little skin
water bag had come out of another pocket in the
sark. The girl wanted to reach for it, but hesitated,
unwilling to remove her hand from her breast.

"Child, what are you holding?" the duarough
asked, setting down the water bag and leaning
closer. "Will you show me?"

The upperlander drew back. The pearl was her
secret, its wan glow visible only in near total darkness. Not even the Bird had known she had it, the
terrible black bird that had...A sharp twinge
behind her ear warned her away. Hastily, she
shoved the almost-memory aside and stared at the
duarough. Surely she could trust Maruha. Slowly,
she drew back her hand. Beneath the yellow fabric

of her gown, the clear blue light shone constant white.

The duarough gasped. "What is that? Did you find it here in the caves?"

The girl shook her head, making bold to follow the other's words a little now. The duarough reached for the pearl.

"May I see it, child?"

The upperlander's hand clapped down again, covering her treasure.

"Hi— migh— mine!" she gabbled. No words came out, only fragments. Maruha drew back.

"Very well, child. I'll not disturb it. But I've never seen the like. You never found it in these caves, I'll vow. Had it with you all along, I'll wager, and we never even noticed."

She lifted her fingerlamp from the floor and held it up so that its strong, dancing light drowned out the pearl's cool, gentle one. The red-haired duarough got to her feet and brushed the cave grit from her trousers distractedly. She donned the fingerlamp again.

"Wonders upon wonders," she murmured. "Who *are* you, girl?"

But the upperlander could not answer. Already the sense of the other's words was fading. She could no longer follow. A fog covered her thoughts. She was very tired. Maruha pulled her to her feet.

"We had best get back. I left those two fools at the camp, though they wanted to help me search. I told them they would as likely fright you away again as find you."

As Maruha started down the corridor, the pale girl hesitated.

"Come. All's well," said the duarough, turning. "I've forbidden Brandl any more barding. He won't frighten you again."

She let Maruha draw her away down the dark and narrow hall.

THEY WERE NEARING WHERE MARUHA said the camp must be. All the corridors looked the same to the girl. The duarough called out a greeting, but only silence answered.

"That's odd," she murmured.

She had extinguished her fingerlamp, since the pearl gave a more constant light, with none of the jump and shadow of flame. Maruha quickened her step until, rounding the bend, she halted dead. The campsite lay in disarray, the cooking lamp overturned and deep ruts in the sand, as though made by running, slipping feet. The duarough hurried forward, pulling the girl along.

"This was not the way I left them!" Maruha exclaimed. "They had put the camp back in good order after you fled. Collum? Brandl?"

Only stillness replied. Collum's pack rested far off to one side, as though dragged there, or thrown. Tools lay scattered about. Brandl's harp gleamed, tilted upside down against one tunnel wall. Maruha caught it up in passing, then fell to her knees beside the upturned cooking lamp.

"Ravenna preserve us," she whispered. "I should never have left them! We are in strange territory, long deserted by our folk. None of our wards operate here, and no telling what is loose in these halls."

Frantically she snatched up Collum's tools, throwing them willy-nilly into the pack along with the harp and the cooking lamp. She slung the strap over one shoulder beside her own and grasped the pale girl's hand again.

"The sand is so dry and scattered, I cannot find a good print. The lamp's still half full. This could not have happened long ago at all. We heard nothing of struggle, but these twisting tunnels distort the sound."

Reaching into her sleeve pocket, she pulled out a dirk, slim and narrow shafted—more stiletto than dagger—with a hollow point. It gleamed in the light. Astonished, the upperlander drew back from it: ugly, poison-filled weapon. It reminded her of what the black bird had carried in its bill.... Maruha paid no attention, only pulled her along hard behind.

"Hurry, child," the stout little woman urged. "Brandl and Collum are doubtless in jeopardy. I only pray we are not too late!"

SNARLS AND COUGHLIKE BARKING, THE scratch of boots on sand and the grunt of men hard-pressed quickened Maruha's pace to a hurtling run. She dragged the pale girl after her down the wide white corridors. A jumping lampflame and shadows on the wall around a sharp turn in the tunnel made the duarough catch in her breath. Rounding the corner, she dropped the upperlander's hand.

The girl stumbled to a halt. They stood at the junction of several corridors. All looked old and unused, the masonry of the arches crumbling. She saw Collum and Brandl with their backs to a blank stretch of wall, cornered by the snapping, snarling creatures that crouched sinuously before them. Brandl had a shortsword, Collum a hollow dirk like the one Maruha held. Both men wore fingerlamps, holding them high for light and occasionally driving back their attackers with fire instead of blade.

The creatures that had cornered them were large and white with stubby legs: two before, two behind, with an extra pair at midbody. Their blunt snouts emitted a doglike coughing. Patches of black masked their fierce red eyes and tipped their long, thick, tapering tails. They traveled low to the ground, their bodies so long that they humped in the middle. Their gait was an odd, fluid undulation, deceptively agile. There were nearly a dozen of them. The upperlander recoiled.

"Weaselhounds!" cried Maruha softly. "Part of the Witch's brood."

Flinging off her packs, she rushed forward and stung one of the creatures from behind with her dirk. It turned like a whiplash to snap at her. Maruha stung it again across the muzzle. It shrank away, scratching its mask with long-nailed paws. The pale girl stood mesmerized, not daring to move.

Before her, too hard-pressed to look up, Collum and Brandl seemed not to have noticed Maruha yet. One weaselhound leapt and caught hold of Brandl's sleeve. He brought his fingerlamp down on its skull with a crack. The white creature released its grip, but the impact had jarred loose the lamp. It fell to the floor and went out. One of the beasts seized it in its jaws and slung it away. Collum cursed.

He drove his hollow dirk into the neck of one of the animals as it lunged for his leg. The creature gave a yip and sprang back, shaking its head. Then it stumbled and sank. Two of its fellows dragged its still form out of their path and plunged again at the duarough men. The weaselhound Maruha had stung now lay still as well. She waded forward and pricked another on the ear.

"Maruha!" Collum looked up in startled disbelief. His joy quickly vanished. "It's no good—there are too many...."

"Save yourself!" Brandl shouted above the growling. "We'll hold them as long as we can—"

"I will not," Maruha flung back, kicking one of the weaselhounds in the ribs so that it turned and pricked itself upon her poisoned dagger. It sprang away with a yelp. Its fellows, aware of the duarough woman now, turned on her.

"Run, Maruha. It's hopeless!" cried Brandl.

He stumbled backward into Collum beneath the furious onslaught of two of the 'hounds. Collum lost his footing in the fallen masonry. As his arm struck the cave wall, his lamp, too, went out. All three of them gasped, as though expecting to be plunged into darkness, but the cool, steady light of the pearl now filled the chamber. The duaroughs looked up, and the weaselhounds turned suddenly, all of them, to stare.

The pale girl stood shaking. The Witch's creatures terrified her—yet they seemed arrested by her light. Unsteadily, she reached into her garment and drew out the pearl, so that its wan glow might shine more strongly. The pin behind her ear pricked warningly, but the red eyes of the weaselhounds frightened her more than the prospect of pain. The light, she realized, would hold them at bay.

As if sensing her defiance, the pin bit down viciously until she gasped—but she refused to return the jewel to its hiding place. Gritting her teeth, the upperlander held up the pearl. Circling, watching her every move, the Witch's beasts began to yip and howl. They cowered before the pearl's dim blue light. Maruha stabbed two with her poisoned dirk before they slunk snarling into the nearest of the tunnels. Collum and Brandl stood open mouthed. Though the pain intensified with every step, the girl forced herself to follow the weaselhounds, herding them.

Whining and snapping, the Witch's brood retreated farther down the hall. Drawing his pick,

Collum sprang onto the pile of rubble that lay to one side of the tunnel's collapsing arch. Barely short of the entryway, the pale girl halted, panting with the effort of defying the pin and gazing after the snapping 'hounds that milled and paced just beyond the first intensity of the light. Collum struck the keystone of the arch.

"Get back, girl!" Brandl cried, rushing forward.

Above them, the arch collapsed with a roar. The upperlander clutched the pearl to her as Brandl shoved her clear. She lay on the hard ground a moment then, her head still one great throbbing ache. Choking, the young duarough held his sleeve over his nose. Collum threw a handful of something into the air, and in a moment, the dust abruptly settled. From the other side of the rubble, the girl heard the weaselhounds gargling and digging. Bruised and shaken, she straightened. Brandl picked himself up, still staring at her.

"What is that light, that jewel she carries?"

Maruha shook her head. Collum was kneeling beside her, examining a wound on her wrist. The sleeve was bloody, torn. "It's nothing," she told him and pulled away. Then, to Brandl, "I know not. But it can be nothing Witch-made, that I vow, since her creatures shun it."

She knelt, rekindling fingerlamps, handing Brandl his harp and Collum his pack.

"Do you still say she must be one of the Witch's?" she demanded tartly. The bearded duarough flushed.

"I know not what she is," he answered at last. "But I know she has saved us this day."

Brandl put up his shortsword and stowed the harp. He glanced uneasily at the new-made wall. "That'll not last long against their claws."

Shaking, the upperlander put away the pearl. The pain in her head did not subside. Angrily, she stood. She was tired of this blankness of memory and the torment of the pin—tired of being terrorized and controlled! Who was she? How had she come here? She needed answers. Wincing, she ignored the pain and surveyed the scene around her.

The concussion of the tumbling arch had shaken loose other stones as well. The blank wall against which Collum and Brandl had made their stand was cracked now with a spiderweb of fissures. Near the ceiling, a slab of plaster had sheared away to reveal a great starburst carved into the stone. It occurred to the pale girl that most of this wall might be plaster, not stone at all.

"But which path?" Maruha was saying. "If

weaselhounds are afoot, you can be sure all the paths hereabouts are overrun with them."

The girl moved nearer, drawn to the starburst. The pin throbbed ever more fiercely, but furiously she disregarded its signal to retreat. As she lifted one finger to touch the starburst, the fissure below it deepened, and a crumbling brick of dried clay fell with a thunk, leaving a hole in the wall. Darkness and emptiness lay beyond, and the scent of stale air. Collum was fishing for the map in his sark. Unfolding it, he and Maruha bent over it. The pale girl grimaced as the pin twisted down. Defiantly, she pulled another brick from the wall.

"This way leads on to other paths, as do these," the duarough woman murmured.

"They could lead to weaselhounds as well. . . ."

With growing determination, the girl dug more bricks from the opening. The pain was nearly blinding now, but she kept on. Despite the heavy cost, she found that thwarting the pin brought her an immense satisfaction. Though it could still torture her, the Witch's weapon no longer possessed her will.

The wall's opening was now wide enough to admit the upperlander's head and shoulders. Leaning through, she felt a sudden peace washing over her, better than food or drink or rest. She halted, stunned as the pain behind her ear abruptly ceased. Before her, the pearl's light revealed a very broad, straight corridor stretching away into the distance. The walls were carved with figures of duaroughs and machines.

"Whatever path we take, let us take it quickly," Brandl, behind her, was urging.

Carefully, the pale girl glanced around. If she removed her head from the opening, she knew, the pain of the pin would return. His back to her, Brandl eyed the shifting rubble of the rockfall nervously. The growling of weaselhounds and the sound of their digging on the other side grew more vigorous. Collum bent over his fingerlamp, trimming the wick. Neither of them took any notice of the girl.

"No path is safe," Maruha told them, rattling the map one-handed in exasperation and nursing her wounded arm. "We must choose one and go."

Without another moment's hesitation, the upperlander turned from the duaroughs and crawled through the opening into the adjoining corridor. *Here!* she wanted to call. Here lay the path they must take. But the pin still prevented her from speaking—even if it could no longer cause her pain. The ceiling overhead rose beyond her reach. The carvings ran in a low, narrow band along either wall. The Shadow would never find her here. She was certain of it. Faintly behind her, she heard Brandl cry out.

"Where's the girl?"

Maruha gave a shout. Their voices sounded remote, like words whispered into a copper bowl. Curses. The sound of bustling.

"She was standing just there—" Brandl started, then: "Look!"

Exclamations. Murmuring. Silence.

"A false wall!" That was Maruha. "Boost me up, Collum, so I can see."

Scrabbling. The girl turned to glimpse the duarough woman staring at her through the hole. She smiled at Maruha, trying to show them by her expression what she could not put into words: what a miraculous place this was. Her serene feeling of contentment grew. They would all find what they were seeking here—or if not quite *here*, then somewhere very close at hand. Perhaps at the end of the corridor. Maruha vanished. A frantic rattling of parchment.

"That's Ravenna's Path," Collum was exclaiming. "One of the pilgrims' roads to the City of Crystalglass! See, it's marked here on the map. It must have been walled off when the City was sealed."

"It's very wide and straight, with beautiful carving along the walls. The girl's in there," said Maruha.

"Let's follow her, then," Brandl hissed, "and seal it after us: quick! Before the 'hounds break through. We can hide in there until they move on."

Scrabbling again. The youngest duarough wriggled through the hole and dropped to the ground with a breathless *oof.* He glanced at the girl, who smiled radiantly back. He stared a moment, obviously puzzled, then shook his head as if too pressed to wonder at it now. But she noted a trace of a smile beginning to tug at his own lips, as though he, too, were starting to feel the strange tranquillity of the pilgrims' road. Picking himself up and turning to stand on toes, he called cheerfully back to Maruha and Collum.

"Pass me the bricks and the packs!"

Smiling still, the pale girl turned away from him and wandered down the hall, aware of a gentle, inexorable tug pulling her on. A Call. Sweet, eerie euphoria continued to steal over her. She ran her fingers along the wall carvings: small, squat figures that were surely duaroughs, here and there taller figures like herself, and occasionally one very much taller than the rest—human-shaped, but strangely garbed.

They all meant nothing to her, but she felt sure now that all her questions would be answered if only she could discover the source of that which summoned her. Behind her, Collum had boosted Maruha through the crack and let her pull him up after. The two of them stood furiously shoving clay bricks back into place, while Brandl, grinning ecstatically himself now, exclaimed in wonder, holding his fingerlamp up before the frieze. The girl kept moving, farther and farther from the false wall and the duaroughs.

"No, wait. It's no good!" Brandl cried suddenly, his smile washing away. "The 'hounds will know we're in here—they'll follow our scent."

"Not if we confuse their senses," replied Maruha grimly.

Glancing back, the upperlander saw her drawing from her sark a glass ampoule. Brandl retreated swiftly. Kneeling on Collum's shoulders, Maruha shook the amber globe, then tossed it through the last brickhole. The girl glimpsed a phosphorescent flash. Coughing and shielding her nose with her sleeve, Maruha shoved the last brick into place and jumped down. Collum guided her after Brandl. Presently a stink like rotten toad-stools drifted past. Uninterested, the pale girl turned away.

Come. The Call reached out to her down the broad corridor: *Come.*

FOUR

Crystalglass

❧

COLLUM AND BRANDL SWUNG THEIR PICKS, chipping furiously at a round metal aperture in the low ceiling above their heads. They were no longer in the broad pilgrims' hall, but in a smaller, narrower way. Though the duaroughs' initial plan had been only to hide and wait, the fantastical carvings upon the walls of the pilgrims' road had drawn them on and on. The Call had begun to affect them, too—though not so strongly as the girl. The pale upperlander refused to stop, even when Maruha stumbled, faint with wound fever, and Collum and Brandl had to support her between them.

"Stay with the girl," Maruha insisted, her voice a croak.

They had come upon more weaselhounds—

even there, on Ravenna's Path. Luckily only a pair of them this time, which Collum and Brandl laid low in a rush. Thereafter, the duaroughs kept a constant, darting watch. When the upperlander, oblivious to all protests and entreaties, turned off the main way into a little side corridor, they had no choice but to follow—for the inexorable Call tugged at them all and allowed them no rest.

Still the girl smiled, padding relentlessly on. They were all but carrying Maruha by then. When they heard gargling and barking in the passageway behind, accompanied now by a deeper, inhuman grunting and snuffling, Brandl's eyes widened.

"Is it ... ?" He glanced at Collum, who nodded grimly.

"Aye, lad. Trolls. No eyes and twice again our size—they hunt by scent alone."

Maruha managed to raise her bowed head from her breast. "We must find an exit soon, or we're all done for," she whispered. "Blind trolls won't shun the pale girl's light."

But for the moment, they could only bolt deeper into the unknown tunnel. The narrow side passage wormed through the stone without intersection. Cursing between their teeth, the duaroughs had soon outstripped the girl, whose pace never quickened, never slackened. Now they worked desperately at the metal portal overhead, its surface overgrown with hard lime and stone daggers. It was the first exit they had found—was, in fact, their only chance of escape, for the corridor ended a half dozen paces beyond.

"Perish the lime," Collum grated. "Wherever this leads, it hasn't been used in years."

A great mass of stone daggers peeled from the aperture's rim under the onslaught of his pick and shattered on the floor. Behind him, Maruha groaned and wiped her brow with her sleeve. She reclined to one side, breathing shallowly, her wounded arm cradled to her breast. The flesh of her wrist was puffed and red, her face flushed.

"Just as well," she answered hoarsely, "or likely they'd have sealed it properly."

She cast an exhausted, harried glance back down the corridor. The sound of shrill, whistled baying and low, throaty whuffling was louder now. Brandl struck off another dagger, and Maruha weakly tugged the upperlander back as it, too, broke upon the floor, throwing fragments that rattled against the walls.

"There," Collum said at last. "Let us see if it will turn."

Teeth gritted, he handed his tool to Brandl and grappled with the hub. A little of the stone still encrusting it crumbled, but the cover itself did not budge.

"Odds and blast," he muttered.

Brandl gave Maruha both picks and, gripping the other set of handholds, he added his strength to the older duarough's. They strained again. This time the metal groaned and gradually gave. Slowly, the cover rotated. It screwed out of the ceiling, shrieking, and fell open with a clang. A brief grin lit Collum's face. Brandl laughed. Panting, the bearded duarough dusted his hands off on his breeches. The high-pitched baying down the corridor behind them echoed in the close confines of the tunnel. Approaching footsteps boomed. Collum and Brandl hastily pulled Maruha to her feet.

Silently, the girl moved past them and climbed upward through the hatch. As she emerged, she heard Brandl following. Collum quickly boosted Maruha through, then came himself. A moment later, he pulled the hatch to, and the sound of their pursuers was abruptly cut off. Collum screwed shut the round door and slid a bolt into place to prevent its being turned again from below. The pale girl stood away from the now-sealed opening, her smile broadening. The Call was much stronger here.

Gazing about her, she realized all at once that she stood upon the planet's surface, no longer underground. A vast City surrounded her, like none she had ever seen. Strange, stately buildings of colored glass rose on every side, flanking deserted streets. No carts or foot traffic thronged the broad thoroughfares. No lights shone. No sound came, not even an animal's cry. The City stood silent, dead.

Above her, the sky stretched black, as it always did, night or day. It was night now, for the blinding white jewel of Solstar hung nowhere above the horizon. Only starlight and the ghostly blue face of Oceanus peered down at her through the vast crystal Dome enclosing the City. No wind moved, and the air was thick, heady, hard to breathe. She had never tasted such air before: Ancients' ether.

"By the underreaches of the world," murmured Brandl, gazing about him at the dark, silent, shimmering buildings of colored glass. "No song or story ever told it was like this."

"I've never been aboveground before," whispered Maruha. "Is that the sky? Without the Dome overhead, I'd feel I might float away from the ground."

Collum shuddered and ducked his head. "Be

glad we came up when it's night," he murmured. "If the light of Solstar fell on us, we'd turn to stone. Duaroughs weren't made to bear such light as that."

The pale girl wasn't listening. The Call was irresistible now. She started down the grand street that lay before her. Automatically, the others followed. With the danger of trolls and weaselhounds safely skirted, they too had fallen once more under the influence of the Call. Maruha walked slowly, leaning against Collum, exclaiming time and again over the machinery they passed.

"What was its function? Where did it come from? Who tended it?"

Brandl fingered his harp through the fabric of his pack. "Look at the arches on their doorways!" he whispered. "How tall they must have stood."

The girl paid no attention to anything they said. Turning down a very wide, straight street, she saw at the end of it a great building of green, violet, and indigo glass. A beacon burned in its spire, white and brilliant as Solstar. It was from there that the Call issued. She felt it. Relief and joy filled her. Eagerly, she hurried forward, almost running.

"Look," cried Brandl.

"It's the Ravenna's hall," Maruha said. "It must be."

"Aye, but is the Ravenna even there to be found?" muttered Collum. "Or just her body? The Ancients left bodies when they died, you know. They didn't fall to ash in a few hours' time, like normal folk. Sooth, what makes that light?" he exclaimed. "No oil I know burns so clean and clear."

The pale girl trotted on. The beacon reminded her of a burning crown, of a tower in which she had once stood, watching a great Flame flare....
But the memory slipped away. She focused on the glass palace ahead. The nearer she came to it, the safer she felt. She hastened until she reached the hall: huge and broad based, it seemed to reach up to heaven itself.

A great door, blank as a mirror, stood at the top of wide steps, barring her. The girl halted and stared, astonished. She had expected no impediment. Her own image, dimly reflected in the dark portal's surface, stared back at her: fair and tall and slender still, but not starved or straggling. The sight of herself no longer frightened her.

But she had no time to study it now. She needed to enter the hall—and the door was in the way. When she brushed it with one hand, it sang to her touch. It felt slippery, seeming to vibrate. Confounded, she recoiled from the strange sensation, then pounded the slick, shimmering door once, twice, angrily. The reflections of the three duaroughs gaped at her from the glassy surface. Her fist against the barrier made a dull tonging sound. She scratched with her nails, and the hum sang musically, altering its tone each time she changed the way she struck it.

"Child, stop. Stop!" Maruha cried. "We've no idea what that is—"

Impatiently, the girl shook her off. Nothing mattered but her urgency to reach the source of the silent summons that drew her. She slapped the dark door with the flat of her hand. It tammered like a gong. Brandl tried to take her other arm, but she snatched it from him. Her heel struck the humming surface, low. It boomed this time, a drum.

"She'll bring the wrath of the Ravenna down on us—" Collum started.

"So you *do* believe the Ancientlady may still live," panted Maruha with some satisfaction.

"Help me," Brandl exclaimed, trying to get hold of her again. "She's—"

He broke off abruptly. All four of them stopped, the three duaroughs falling back. Only the pale girl remained planted, staring as, upon the surface of the barrier, the head and shoulders of a man—much larger than life—suddenly shivered into being. His face was broad, with strong, high cheeks, his nose flattened and the nostrils flared. His skin was very dark, his tightly curled hair peppered with grey. He was wearing what might have been a tunic, black and silver. He seemed startled, disconcerted, and therefore fierce.

"Who knocks so at the port?" he demanded. "This City is closed."

His countenance alarmed the girl, but she glared back at the image, unable to answer. The three duaroughs came forward hesitantly.

"We...we seek the counsel of the Ravenna," Maruha began. "We have an upperlander who needs her aid."

The image of the man frowned and studied them. "Many need our aid," he answered presently, "but we cannot give it. Weightier matters occupy us. Do you not know of our instructions that no one is to disturb this City until we ourselves reopen it? How did you enter? The airlocks are barred."

"If by airlocks you mean gates leading to the desert outside—" Collum stammered. He looked terrified. "We did not come that way. We came by underpaths. We are duaroughs."

"I can see that," the dark man's image snapped.

"We thought all those gates sealed as well, and the service ports. I'm surprised the alarms didn't sound. No matter. By whatever path you entered, take yourselves off by the selfsame—"

"But we can't!" Brandl cried. "There are weaselhounds and trolls."

The other sighed in agitation. "Yes, of course. Oriencor's brood. I'd forgotten. Very well. I will open one of the airlocks for you and let you out into the desert."

"We'll turn to stone when Solstar rises!" Collum exclaimed.

"We'll starve," Brandl beside him said.

"Please, sir," Maruha begged. She was panting again, holding her injured arm, near the end of her strength. "We must see the Ravenna. This girl has the Witch's pin behind her ear—"

"That is not our concern!" the dark man's image answered sharply. "We cannot attend to you."

The pale girl growled. Desperate rage welled in her. She struck the man's image with the heel of her hand. The stone vibrated with a dull thrum, and the picture shimmered for a moment before reforming. His features flinched in surprise, then clouded with anger.

"Pardon, sir," Maruha cried hurriedly. "She is

a child and has been injured by the Witch. Let us in, we beg you. The Ravenna…"

"Has seen no one from outside the Dome in a thousand years." The man's black eyes turned on her impatiently. "Now be off. I will not admit you."

Collum and Brandl shifted uneasily. Baring her teeth, the girl prepared to fly at him again.

"But you must," Maruha pleaded.

"No!" the other began.

"Yes, Melkior," another voice cut in quietly. "You must." The words were low and musical, a woman's voice. The pale girl relaxed even as the three duaroughs started and cast about, for the speaker was nowhere to be seen. The image of the dark man, too, glanced startled to one side. "Admit them, Melkior," the deep, sweet voice of the unseen speaker said. "I will aid them."

THE GIRL STOOD ALONE IN A SUMPTUOUS room. How long since she had entered the great hall through the black doorway, she did not know—an hour? Two? After the woman's words, the dark, shimmering force that had buzzed and barred them abruptly vanished. Presently Melkior—the man himself—had appeared, life-sized now, no longer the great magnified image. Nevertheless he was very tall, towering over the pale girl. The duaroughs came scarcely to his sash. He led them in graciously enough, but with his mouth tight, brow furrowed in agitation.

The girl followed him eagerly down long, empty corridors, past dark, glinting galleries. In some of them, lights moving in the walls were making patterns: rose, yellow, violet, green. Nowhere were any lamps lit or any windows to be seen, but the darkness of the hall did not unease her. They met no one. Abruptly, their guide had halted, turning toward one wall. It parted like a curtain as he touched it, and the girl moved past him into the chamber beyond.

The air within was cool and strangely scented, but the floor beneath her feet was warm. It was utterly black, like noon sky between the stars. Curtains of pale gauze draped the windowless walls. As with the rest of the palace, the walls were made of glass: dark blue and rippled, it seemed to harbor a low inner fire that now and again coalesced into little strands of burning color.

The Call was overwhelming here. It surrounded her, equally strong on every side. She waited now, only remotely aware of the dark man barring the duaroughs from joining her, of Maruha's startled protests, broken off as the wall seamed shut. She stood alone, feeling the coolness of the air and the warmth of the black glass floor underfoot, gazing absently at the colored sparks winking and darting through the ultramarine walls.

The air in the room shifted, and she turned to see a very tall figure entering the chamber. The portal closed soundlessly behind the woman. Her silver slippers whispered on the floor. She stood even taller than the dark man had. Her features resembled his: high cheekbones, a broad flat nose and generous mouth, but her skin was dusky, not black. Her eyes were deeply blue. She was wearing a robe of jet and indigo. Her hair, dark and wavy, with silver threads, hung unbound behind her. She paused just inside the chamber, surveying the pale girl for a long moment with blue and lionlike eyes.

"Do you know me, child?" she said at last, her voice very low and full of the music the girl remembered hearing at the greathall's outer door. The tall woman drew closer through the twilight. Her face, though unlined, gave the impression of great age, and her bearing, though upright, of great weariness. "So the pilgrims' Call has brought you to me," she said. "I am glad you have come."

But she sighed saying it. The pale girl looked at her. The other's face, full of welcome, seemed also strangely sad.

"What are you hiding beneath your hand?"

The girl felt not the slightest fear or urge to draw away. She considered only a moment before lifting her hand from her breast. The pearl's soft light shone through the fabric of her gown. Around them, light seemed to gather in the walls, the beads of fire brightening. The dark lady smiled.

"A lampwing's egg," she murmured, "already kindled! Oh, that is well, for none but a corundum shell can hold what I must give you. May I see it?"

Without hesitation, the pale girl drew out the shining thing. The dusky woman took it in her palm and passed her other hand over it. The pale girl started, frowning, stared. Her pearl had vanished.

"Don't fear," said the other gently. "I have it safe, and you will have it back soon, I promise. Now let me look at your head. I want to see what the Witch has done to you."

The pale girl did not flinch but bowed her head and let the lady's great, delicate hands comb carefully through her hair. They stopped suddenly. She heard the other's indrawn breath.

"I see it now."

The music of the other's voice was more soothing to the pale girl than water. She kept her eyes closed, her forehead resting against the tall woman's breast. The other sighed. She did not touch the pin, only kept one hand lightly on the girl's head, cradling it. The dark, rare fragrance that came to the girl from the other's hair, her robe, was like damp earth and flowers never before scented or known.

"But tell me how it came to pass that you allowed the Witch to put a pin behind your ear. You must have dropped your guard very low to have allowed her that—for she is terrified of you, my green-eyed girl, ever since you stole one of her darkangels in Avaric and made him a man again."

She heard the other laugh softly, stroking her brow. The words evoked no memories, but she loved the touch of those hands. They were cool and silky dry and smelled of myrrh. This heavier air bore scents—sounds, too—so much more richly than the thin stuff outside the Dome.

Gently, the woman lifted her head. Dark blue eyes searched the girl's.

"Such green eyes you have, child. Corundum mingled with the gold, so that magic is as drawn to you as beebirds to wedding trumps."

The pale girl closed her eyes, breathing in the heady fragrance of the lady and the room.

"Can you talk at all, child?" the dark lady asked her.

The girl ducked her head. She could not speak, did not want to, did not want to try.

"Try," the tall woman urged. "Let me see how deep the pin has bit."

The pale girl shivered. "Uh," she managed, a dull and ugly sound. "Uhn, mmh."

The other frowned. "Deep, I see."

"Mmh," the pale girl muttered. "Ngh."

One hand left her cheek. She sensed it hovering above the pin.

"Cold as winterock," the dark lady whispered. "Feel how it chills the air! There can be no leaving it, then. Rest your head against me, child."

Gratefully, the girl pressed her cheek to the rich fabric of the other's robe. Some of it felt slick and cool, like wet leaves. Other places were warm and napped, like stone moss or mouse's fur. She nestled closer.

"Peace," the tall woman told her. "Be still."

All at once, without warning, the girl felt the pin seized and twisted, plucked suddenly free. The air gave a crackling hiss, smelled acrid of scorching. Then pain rushed into the wound like a flood of fire. Screaming, the girl tore herself from the other's grasp. The dark lady stood, holding the pin up between thumb and forefinger. It was over three inches long, with a crossguard near the blunt end, like a tiny sword. White flame danced along its length. Its point gleamed, wet and red.

The tall woman reached out to her, her expression full of compassion and horror and grief. With a shriek, the pale girl fended her off. Her own hand came away from her head covered in blood. The room seemed full of brightness now, the fiery pain consuming her. She felt as though her whole being might burn away in the flash. And she was screaming still—but no longer because of the pain. She was screaming because she remembered now. She remembered everything.

FIVE

Aeriel

～

HER NAME WAS AERIEL. SHE REMEMBERED
now: born in Pirs, heir to the suzerain there, then
sold into slavery after her father's overthrow. And
she remembered the darkangel, swooping down on
his dozen black pinions to carry her away.

On Avaric's white plain,
where an icarus now wings...

The words ran through her mind like an in-
cantation. She recalled the wedding sari she had
donned in marriage to the darkangel—how, to
dissolve the evil enchantment upon him, she had
surprised him with a magic cup made from the
hoof of a dead starhorse:

Then strong-hoof of a starhorse
        must hallow him unguessed
If adamant's edge is to plunder
        his breast.

Using the keen edge of an unbreakable blade, she had extracted the darkangel's leaden heart and given him her own to make him mortal again. Once free of the Witch's spell, Prince Irrylath had turned in horror against his former mistress and begun raising an army to destroy her.

Then, only, may the Warhorse
        and Warrior arise
To rally the warhosts, and thunder
        the skies.

Aeriel, meanwhile, had traversed half the nations of Westernesse to rescue the lost lons, once guardians of the world, who had been turned into gargoyles by the Witch—for without these powerful allies, Aeriel knew, her husband's burgeoning warhost had little hope of victory.

"What befell you then," the dark lady said, "once you had rescued my lons at Orm, and stood in the temple Flame, and burned your shadow away?"

Aeriel could not see her questioner. The Ancient's voice seemed to come from the air. She felt as though she were floating, suspended in nothing. She heard another voice as well: murmuring, telling everything, and realized presently it was her own. Images of whatever she remembered and spoke aloud swirled before her in the darkness in little running beads of fire.

"After Orm, we departed for Isternes," she murmured.

"Where the great conclave was held?"

Aeriel nodded. "Yes." The pictures of fire strung themselves before her on the darkened air. "But first the women-of-learning and the magic-men brought forth the starhorse."

"Who had been dead," the other prompted. "Who had been killed years ago by the dark-angel."

"The priestesses said they could rebuild the Horse," Aeriel replied, "call back his wandering soul and revive him in new flesh, the very image of the old, with memory of his former life and death."

"Did they succeed?" the Ancient persisted. "Tell me."

"Oh, yes," Aeriel breathed, the memory-scene

unfolding before her, clear as though it were this very moment happening. She nodded. "The star-horse. Yes. I remember him."

THE CROWD HAD STOOD FLOCKED IN THE great square before the Istern palace, all the people with their plum-colored skin, the women in their turbans and flowing trousers, the men in their long gowns, heads veiled against the white, slant morning light of Solstar. Syllva, the Lady of Isternes, stood foremost, flanked upon one side by Irrylath, her son. Aeriel stood beside him. Craning eagerly, Irrylath's half brothers—the Lady's younger sons—stood opposite. A glimpse, a murmur from the throng, and the priestesses led forth the star-horse. Aeriel's heart leapt at the beauty of him: Avarclon, the guardian of Avaric.

She felt her husband shiver hard, though with delight or terror at the sight, she could not tell. Irrylath no longer shunned her, as he had for the first year of their marriage. Nor did he shrink from her now. But he had seemed in awe of her since Orm: she suspected he found her presence troubling, even painful. *Why?* The question needled her, and she had no clue. Always he treated her more as some distant, valued ally than as his wife or even a friend. An overwhelming sense of failure ate at her, for Irrylath was her husband only in name.

Overcome by longing, Aeriel pressed nearer to him, using the crush of the crowd as an excuse. He appeared oblivious to her, his gaze directed toward the starhorse, who came forth from the temple all silver fire. Those hooves, striking the paving stones, were throwing white sparks. Great wings—the pair that sprang from the Horse's withers—arched, flexing, and beat the air, while his little wings—those that dressed his fetlocks and adorned his cheeks—fluttered. He tossed his tail. He pranced, and one hoof shone brighter than the rest, dazzling in the light of Solstar.

Aeriel sensed Irrylath beside her growing taut, his breath quickening. She felt his back arch, his own shoulders flex as Avarclon's pinions beat. Was he remembering his own wings, a dozen of them, that he had worn as a darkangel? Now it was Aeriel who shivered. Her husband had ceased to be that powerful wingèd creature not by his own choice, but by hers. What must it be like, she wondered, to have lost such wings? Avarclon tossed his head, his brow-horn cutting the air. His nostrils flared, and he whinnied a long, trumpeting call.

"By Ravenna, who first made me," he cried, shaking himself, "it is a fine match. A new body as like my old as could be. You have done well, priests and wisewomen, in building this new engine for my soul. I thank you. It is good to be in the world again."

His eyes like bright meteors scanned the crowd.

"Companions," he called to his fellow guardians, the lons, "you who were with me at our first making, I greet you. That you are all assembled can mean but one thing, that you have been rescued from the Witch's power as I was from death, and the war against her is on."

The great lyon Pendarlon roared in answer. "Yes, you have it, friend."

The starhorse turned his head and gazed upon the Lady of Isternes. She went to him. "Ah, Lady," he said, "king's wife in Avaric. I rejoice to see you again. What is this place?"

"This is my land," the Lady Syllva replied, "that you would call Esternesse. Once wife to the late king of Avaric—yes, I was. But no more. I am returned again to my own dominion."

The starhorse bowed his head. "I remember now. I saw your train departing after the death of your son."

"You mistake," Syllva replied. "He did not die."

Aeriel could not see her face, but from her voice, she knew the Lady must be smiling—as though she told of joyous things. Irrylath caught his breath in through his teeth. Aeriel saw only the side of his face, gone tense and pale.

"He became the Witch's prisoner," the Lady continued undismayed, without a trace of shame, "and she made him into a darkangel."

"A darkangel?" the Avarclon exclaimed, snorting and half rearing. "Little Irrylath that used to sit laughing on my back, and dig at me with his heels for spite and pull my hair?"

Syllva nodded. "But he has been rescued by her who rescued both you and the gargoyles. He is mortal again, and stands at hand."

She turned to her son as she said it, and the equustel, following the line of her sight, cast his silver eyes upon the prince, who flinched beneath that cool and level gaze. Aeriel no longer felt him breathe. The starhorse whickered darkly, low.

"You might be he," he said at last, "that was my Irrylath. Are you also he that put me out of Avaric?"

Aeriel felt her husband shudder. He nodded slowly.

"How came you by those scars upon your cheek?" said Avarclon. "You were fair to look at once."

She felt him draw a ragged breath. Without thinking, she started to take his hand—but then she did think, and did not dare. She heard a rumble from the lyon of the desert behind her. The prince's glance flicked that way for an instant, passing over her without a thought. He turned back to the equustel.

"Pendarlon," he whispered.

The lon of Avaric turned his head and eyed the young man sidelong, sidling. "I died a hard death in exile because of you," he said. "I loved you once."

Irrylath sank down, and Aeriel feared at first he must be faint or falling—but then she realized he was kneeling before the equustel.

"Avarclon," he said. "So much has befallen since I was young and rode your back and pulled your hair, that I hardly know whether I can love you or anyone ever again. But I remember loving you—before the White Witch had me and made me what I was. Of all the wrong I did while in that shape, I swear it was killing you that was the worst. I did not know you then, or know myself. But I face you now and know you.

"I no longer serve the Witch. The wedding toast I drank from your hoof has freed me of her enchantment. I have sworn to overthrow her now, to cast down and unmake her and all her darkangels. But I need a steed. Each of your fellow lons has accepted one of my brothers as a rider. But now no mount remains for me. Will you aid me? I beg you. Let me ride you again as once we rode. Be my ally for a daymonth, a year—and at the end of this war, I shall be yours, to do with as you will."

Aeriel paled, staring at the prince. A kind of roaring filled her ears. At the end of this war, she had had such hopes—that Irrylath might consent to be *hers* at last: her own true husband, her love. A bitter taste came into her mouth. Her balance swayed. *Irrylath, Irrylath,* she wanted to cry. But Irrylath had forgotten her. Shaken, she said nothing, eyeing the kneeling prince of Avaric. He had bowed his head. The starhorse was coming forward to touch his nose to the young man's brow.

"A truce then," said the lon, very softly. "As you wish. Until the Witch be overthrown. Then, make no mistake, I will have my due—but no matter! We will not think of that now. Come take the air with me, king's son of Avaric. Let me see if you still remember how to ride."

Irrylath looked up. Aeriel heard his indrawn breath, saw a joy almost too strong to bear break over his face. He leapt up, catching the starhorse's mane. The silver steed danced back, his great wings stroking as if to tease the prince. Then he turned, and in a bound, Irrylath was astride him. With a mighty leap, the starhorse launched himself and sped away upon the air, circling and climbing above the square while the crowd cried out, craning to see.

Few had heard what had passed between the starhorse and the prince, Aeriel knew—perhaps she alone had heard—and only she could not rejoice. She watched her husband soaring overhead, horse and rider swooping and diving together in dizzying arcs. She could see the prince's face, even at this distance, suffused with rapture still. Was it the wind, the sensation of flight, she wondered, or having won an old friend's forgiveness, if only for a while, or that he and his brothers might now ride against the Witch with some hope of success?

Aeriel only knew that once more he had turned away from her. She felt one hot tear spill before dashing the others angrily aside. She refused to weep openly, here under public gaze. A hand slipped quietly into hers. Startled, she turned. Her friend Erin stood beside her: a tall, spare girl with skin black as night. Her eyes, like jet, found Aeriel's. The dark girl pressed her hand. Of all this great, sprawling throng, Aeriel realized, only Erin was not watching the prince and his steed wheeling and tumbling overhead. Only Erin had eyes for Aeriel.

"AND AFTER THE CONCLAVE?" THE AN-cientlady asked.

Her voice was quiet, patient, but pressing. Aeriel sensed that she must waste no time. She still could not see her questioner. All remained in darkness save for the heatless swirl of fire, but she had now become aware that it was not upon the air that the fire beads danced, but in the depths of a great glass globe that floated before her.

"We set sail across the Sea-of-Dust for the lands of Westernesse," she murmured. "We were joined by the people of Erin's islands in their little skiffs. They have been alone upon the Sea so long, their language is hardly like ours anymore. They look at Erin, who was raised apart from them, and try to speak to her, but she doesn't understand."

"And when you reached the Westron shore?"

"We were met by Sabr, the bandit queen, whom many still call the queen of Avaric. Her followers are brigands—honest people once, who

fled the coming of the darkangel. She is kin to
Irrylath and claimed the crown when the old king
died seemingly without heirs. But she calls Irrylath
her sovereign now."

Aeriel could not keep the bitterness from her
voice. She pictured them, Irrylath and Sabr: two
cousins as like as like. Both were of that lean and
slender build, almost equally tall, with slant eyes
blue as little flames and long, straight black hair
worn in a horsetail down the back. She remembered landfall: Irrylath striding down the gang-
plank, his arms thrown wide to embrace the bandit
queen. Though seemingly cool and reserved by
nature, she had returned his embrace warmly, calling him "cousin" and "lord."

Sabr wore the garb of Avaric: a sark and trousers gathered into boots with upturned toes, a dagger in her belt, a hoop of white zinc-gold piercing
the lobe of one ear. Her face reminded Aeriel un-
cannily of someone—she could not think whom.
Irrylath greeted her with more ardor than Aeriel
had ever seen him display. Of course he knew
Sabr, the daughter of his father's brother. Though
she had not yet been born when he had fallen into
the Witch's power, he had met her not many daymonths past. Finding him near death upon the
drought-stricken shore of Bern, Sabr had nursed

him until he could continue his quest for Aeriel
and the gargoyled lons.

All this he told the Lady Syllva excitedly by
way of introduction. Sabr smiled and allowed the
Lady to kiss her brow. Irrylath introduced his
brothers and their lons, to all of whom she nodded
courteously, followed by Talb the Mage, then
Aeriel's brother, the prince of Pirs—and only then
did he remember Aeriel. Sabr broke off her grave
greeting of the starhorse and turned, a sudden look
of apprehension passing over her oddly familiar
features. Aeriel, too, felt a strange dread at their
meeting, though she could not say why.

"Cousin," Irrylath began, he, too, uneasy
seeming, "this is Aeriel." A pause. More softly,
"My wife."

Sabr put one palm to her shoulder. Head
bowed, the queen of Avaric went down on one
knee before the pale girl in the wedding sari.

"Dread sorceress," she murmured, "deliver us
from the Witch."

Aeriel scarcely caught the words, for she felt
disconcerted, abandoned. Irrylath did not stand by
her, but across from her, alongside Sabr.

"Already you have returned my cousin and the
Avarclon to us," the bandit queen went on, now
lifting her gaze, "for which all Avaric-in-exile re-

joices. Know that my people pledge to serve you in this war."

Aeriel shivered, finding the other's proud blue eyes and the smooth, unmarred surface of her face strangely unnerving. Aeriel shook herself. Everyone was looking at her.

"I accept your fealty, queen of Avaric," she stammered at last, feeling awkward and unprepared—she could scarcely call the woman *queen of bandits* to her face—"and trust that your horsemen and horsewomen will aid us bravely against the Witch. But do not honor me with grand titles, I beg you. I am only Aeriel."

Sabr knelt still, her expression cool and serious and slightly surprised: measuring her, Aeriel realized, as one might a compeer—or a rival. Irrylath said nothing. She found herself holding her breath. No one among the company stirred. Not knowing what to do in the end, Aeriel turned abruptly and left them—prince, bandit queen, and the rest—and tried not to glimpse the look of open relief on her husband's face when he realized she was going.

A DAYMONTH OF MARCHING ENSUED, RE-cruiting, provisioning. How slowly an army moved! Though food was scarce, it was water that was their greatest lack, for the killing drought of the White Witch lay heavy on the land. People came from far and wide, many simply to watch the army pass, but more than a few to join. The allies had gathered contingents from most of the lands of Westernesse—from Bern and nearby Zambul, from northern Pirs, from far Rani and Elver, even Terrain—by the time they reached Pendar. There a dozen tribes of the desert folk waited, among them, the Ma'a-mbai. Aeriel fell into their arms with a joyous cry.

"So, little pale one, you have grown so tall that now they are calling you a sorceress," their leader laughed.

"Chieftess, it is not so," Aeriel said, wiping tears from her eyes. Of all people, truly her old friend the desert wanderer ought to know she was no sorceress. Laughing herself now, she embraced the cinnamon-colored woman. "Oh, Orroto-to, it is good to see you again."

The army continued to grow. When Irrylath's mother, the Lady Syllva, appointed Sabr to lead the forces of the West, the young queen brought her disparate new troops to heel with a swift, sure hand. Each directing one wing of the great army, Sabr and her cousin the prince perfectly mirrored

one another: both proud, intense, aloof. Aeriel
could only admire, even envy, the bandit queen's
easy, almost arrogant assumption of command.

Now they camped at the desert's edge, soon to
set out across the pale amber sands for the distant
Waste and the Witch's Mere. Aeriel felt a growing
anticipation, mingled with dread. She sat with Erin
in the cool lee of a dune. It was nightshade, tents
and pavilions pitched all around them under the
ghostlight of blue Oceanus. Her friend had found
them this quiet spot far from the constant bustle
at the center of the camp. Aeriel was glad to get
away.

"What baffles me," she said, touching the pearl
through the fabric of her gown, "is that we have
seen not one glimpse of the Witch's catspaws in
all the time we have been in Westernesse."

She lifted free the pearl and cupped it in her
hands like a faint, azure coal. Standing in the
temple Flame at Orm had set this lampwing's gift
alight—though its wan glow was difficult to discern except in shadowy darkness such as this,
away from other light. Aeriel shook her head.

"Not one scout nor dog, nor one black bird.
Why has the Witch sent none to spy on us?"

The dark girl laughed, leaning back on one

elbow and poking at the dry sand. "She scarcely needs spies and catspaws to tell her the whereabouts of an army this size."

Aeriel put the pearl away. She felt one corner of her mouth tighten. "Does she not wonder at our number, at our strength?"

Erin found an old bead lying in the sand and held it up. It was deeply reddish, with a hole bored through one end, and carved of sandshell. The dark girl shrugged. "She knows our destination well enough. Perhaps she doesn't care."

"But she *should* care," muttered Aeriel. "This seeming unconcern uneases me."

Erin tossed the blood-colored bead aside and sat up, studying Aeriel. "Perhaps that is her intent, to unease you. This whole business hangs on *you*—somehow."

"On me?" scoffed Aeriel. "Only great good chance has put me where I am."

The dark girl shook her head. "More than chance, my true and only friend. There is a kind of power on you."

"What power have I?" insisted Aeriel. "When Irrylath generals the Lady's Istern troops, Sabr the forces of the West—"

"None of which would now be gathered but for you," Erin cut in gently. "The tales you told and the Torches you lit upon your quest to rescue the gargoyles have awakened half the people in the land. You have opened their eyes to the Witch and shown them the urgency of overthrowing her—today, tomorrow, *soon*—lest we all perish, thirsting to death."

Aeriel ran her hand over the fine, crusted sand. It felt cool and smooth as water in the bright starshine. If only it *were* water, she thought grimly. If the moisture-stealing lorelei were not stopped soon, the whole world would succumb to famine and drought. Again Aeriel shook her head.

"I don't even know the rest of the rime," she murmured, "the rime Ravenna made so long ago to riddle all this out and show us how to unmake the Witch. I only have the first two-thirds."

Leaning back against the dune once more, Erin began to sing in a voice that was low and true:

"On Avaric's white plain,
*　　　　　where an icarus now wings*
To steeps of Terrain
*　　　　　from Tour-of-the-Kings,*

And damozels twice-seven
*　　　　　his brides have all become:*
A far cry from heaven,
*　　　　　a long road from home—*

Then strong-hoof of a starhorse
      must hallow him unguessed
If adamant's edge is to plunder
      his breast.

Then, only, may the Warhorse
      and Warrior arise
To rally the warhosts, and thunder
      the skies."

Aeriel let her mind wander back, remembering how she had found and freed the enchanted lons in the fires of Orm before the Witch's remaining darkangels could recapture them.

"But first there must assemble
      ones icari would claim.
A bride in the temple
      must enter the flame,

With steeds found for six brothers, beyond
      a dust deepsea,
And new arrows reckoned, a wand
      given wings—"

The rime recounted the rescued lons agreeing to serve as steeds for Prince Irrylath's Istern brothers, the magical silver arrowheads forged by Talb the Mage for the Lady Syllva, and the

Ancient white messenger bird that had come to
Aeriel, melding with her wooden staff to become
for a time its living figurehead.

> *"That when a princess-royal's*
> *to have tasted of the tree ..."*

She remembered the taste of a strange golden
fruit upon her tongue—sharp, yet so tremen-
dously sweet. The dark girl sang on:

> *"Then far from Esternesse's*
> *city, these things:*

> *A gathering of gargoyles,*
> *a feasting on the stone,*
> *The Witch of Westernesse's*
> *hag overthrown."*

The gargoyled lons all assembled at Orm, a
dreadful sacrifice upon an Ancient altar, and the
Witch's red-eyed harridan falling screaming from
the highest ledge....

Aeriel came to herself with a start, realizing that
Erin had reached the end of the second long
stanza—the last stanza anyone knew—and had
stopped singing. The pale girl shook herself and
gazed at her friend, wondering.

"Where did you hear that song?" she said. "I never knew it had a tune before."

Erin laughed. "All the camp's singing it. Some bard's doing. Volunteers, when they come, march in singing it. I would not be surprised if it is all over Westernesse by now." She smiled devilishly. "Your notoriety spreads."

Aeriel looked wryly away for a moment—but her annoyance at Erin's playful needling never lasted. She sighed, thinking of the rime. "But what is the rest of it?" she asked. "No one knows. Talb the Mage has no inkling; nor do the lons, and my maiden-spirits have not spoken to me since Orm."

She glanced upward at the constellation of pale yellow stars called commonly the Maidens' Dance. Elliptical in shape, it floated overhead like a burning crown.

"How shall I learn the rest of the rime?" Aeriel wondered aloud. "We're preparing to march, and I don't even know Ravenna's plan!"

Sobering, Erin touched her companion's hand lightly, once. "Take heart. Everything of which the rime speaks so far has come to pass. The Witch must know this. Perhaps she has grown so afraid of you now that she has withdrawn into her palace of cold white stone and will not show herself." The dark girl shrugged. "In all events, it's no use worrying. I am certain that soon you will discover the last of the rime."

Aeriel could not help smiling, just a little. Erin always cheered her. But her mood quickly darkened. She fidgeted, biting her lip.

"It's Irrylath I am most uneasy for. He is still within her reach—and the dreams she sends him are dire. I fear for him."

"I don't," said Erin sourly. "He is so full of his army and this war—he spends more time in the company of Avarclon and that Sabr than he does in yours. He never speaks to you; he does not send for you. Is he not your husband?"

"Peace, Erin," Aeriel said wearily. "There will be time for all that, after the war."

But the dark girl shook her head.

"I have heard the rumors flying all over camp, all about this enchantment the White Witch still holds on him," she exclaimed, "that he may not lie with you or anyone while the White Witch lives—but I tell you from experience that *that* is very little of what makes a man, and though he may not lie with you, he might touch you, or talk to you, or even look at you when you are in his company—but no, it is ever 'my troops,' and 'the warhost,' and 'My steed calls me away!' Sabr, that bedaggered bandit, dotes on him."

Aeriel tensed. "She is his cousin."

"So are you. And which of you is his wife?"

Aeriel felt the knot beneath her breastbone tighten. She gripped a handful of desiccated sand suddenly as though she meant to hurl it at Erin. The near tents sighed in the wind. Aeriel opened her fingers and let the sand trickle away. "I'll not speak of this."

"No, you never will," snapped Erin. She gazed off across the camp, between the airy pavilions in pale, pale green, ghost blue, and mauve. The set of her jaw told Aeriel that her own refusal to speak had hurt her friend.

"It is not...," she began, groping. "It is only that we hardly know one another, Irrylath and I."

Erin looked back at her sidelong. "I have known you far less time than he," she said softly, "and already I love you well."

A stone rose in Aeriel's throat. She put her arms around the dark girl. For a moment, Erin's cheek rested against her breast. "I am so glad you did not go back to your people after Orm," she whispered. "You are my strength. You came on to Isternes for my sake, didn't you?"

Looking up, Erin shook her head and patted Aeriel's cheek. Her palm was cool and dry. "No, dear one," she said. "For mine. I never had a friend before."

She rose.

"But I will leave you now," she said, "for I see you want to be alone. I will be at the campfires of my folk, trying to remember their—*our*—tongue."

Aeriel mustered a smile and let her go. No less confounded than before by the White Witch and by Irrylath, she nonetheless felt easier now for having spoken with Erin. The dark girl bent and kissed her brow.

"But you will forgive me if I think your prince of Avaric a great fool for not loving you," Erin said very gently. "And *you* an even greater one for wanting him to."

SIX

Black Bird

❧

AERIEL AROSE AND WANDERED THROUGH the close-staked pavilions, encountering no one. Those who glimpsed her in the distance gave her a wide berth: all seemed in awe of her. She sighed, lonely suddenly for someone who did not know her, someone who would not recognize her instantly and draw away. She was sorry now to have let Erin leave her, and was just turning to find her way out of the jumble of tentbacks and supply pavilions that surrounded her when a snatch of conversation reached her ear. She paused, frowning, seeing no one else about.

A great green silk tent loomed before her, billowing in the light desert breeze. She felt the air's coolness against her cheek and the touch of the sandy grit it bore. The slapping of the open tent

flap only deepened the stillness. Puzzled, she found
herself listening, straining, but for long moments,
she heard only wind and silk. Then it came again,
a low muffle of voices—one of them unmistakably
Irrylath's.

"If you positioned your horse-troops like
so, my mother's bowwomen could be stationed
here...."

Aeriel froze, hearing the faint rasp of metal
against metal. Another spoke.

"Then our foot could be divided here and
here."

Sabr's voice. She recognized it now, imagined
the bandit queen unsheathing and pointing with
her dagger. The rasp of metal again: the dagger
sheathed.

"You never did tell me what happened to that
fine Bernean blade I once gave you."

A teasing tone had stolen into Sabr's voice.
Aeriel blinked. Banter from the bandit queen was
rare. A rattling of parchment.

"I broke it," came Irrylath's short reply.

Their voices did not come from within, Aeriel
realized suddenly, drawing nearer the dark pavilion. Its back stood close behind the backs of a
rose and a saffron tent, cutting off a kind of courtyard from the open space around.

"How, pray?" the prince's cousin was asking. "The blade was Bernean steel."

Aeriel stood very still beside the green pavilion, listening. Silence from Irrylath. Cautiously, she peered around the green silk edge. Sabr and Irrylath stood in the courtyard beyond. They were alone, without the usual swarm of aides and attendants. Half-turned from his cousin, the prince of Avaric bent over a scroll. Sabr toyed with her own Bernean blade.

"I'll give you another," she told him softly.

"Don't," he said abruptly, straightening and rolling the parchment up.

He moved away from Sabr, but only a step. She followed, and boldly laid one hand—just so—across the scars that threaded his cheek. Astonishment gripped Aeriel. She clenched her teeth to keep from crying out. She expected Irrylath to pull instantly away from Sabr, but instead he turned, slowly, as if unwilling, to look at her.

"Can't you love me, cousin," she asked him, "even a little?"

Aeriel felt a surge of outrage, then blinding jealousy. Irrylath would never have permitted *her* such a touch. She bit her tongue, half hoping he would strike Sabr, push her roughly aside, revile her, but he only shook his head, and the look in his eyes was a desperate sadness, not anger.

"I can love no woman while the Witch's enchantment is on me," he answered. "I have told you that."

He had told her! Incomprehension filled Aeriel. Her fingers on the pole beneath the pavilion silk tightened. She had thought only she and perhaps the Lady Syllva privy to that secret. All Erin and the camp could know were rumors. Yet he had told Sabr. Why? She whom many still called the queen of Avaric dropped her hand from him, her face falling.

"Yes," she said quietly. "And the only satisfaction it gives me is that you cannot love *her* either."

"Don't speak of her so," whispered Irrylath. Sabr turned abruptly away.

"She frightens you, doesn't she?" the prince's cousin snapped. "Almost as much as the Witch. You fear her sorcerous green eyes see everything." Sabr snorted. "Do they? Do they see us now?"

Only half hidden by the corner of the tent, Aeriel stood riveted, too stunned to move. She felt powerless, exposed, standing in plain view. Yet neither her husband nor the so-called queen of Avaric took note of her, their eyes on one another.

"She stood in the temple fire at Orm," continued Sabr bitterly. "It has burned her shadow away. She wears a pearl on her breast that is full of light. What sort of mortal creature is that?"

The bandit queen turned back to Irrylath, seizing his arm. This time he did not move away.

"I tell you, she is no mortal woman! She is some unworldly thing, Ravenna's sorceress. How could you love her? Surely the Witch's spell is simply what you have told her to keep her at bay."

The prince shook his head. His voice was hoarse. "Would that it were."

His cousin did not seem to be listening. Her knuckles were pale where she clenched his arm. "But I *am* a mortal woman. I would be content with just your heart. Truly—"

At last, at last he pulled free of her. Watching, Aeriel held her breath. Her knees felt shaky, weak. She clung to the pavilion pole.

"I am not free to give it," said Irrylath. "My heart is not my own."

"*She* took it, didn't she?" Sabr snapped.

The prince bowed his head, looking away from her. He touched his breast. "And gilded it with lead."

"I wasn't speaking of the Witch," the bandit queen replied. "When *she* rescued you and took the Witch's gilding off, she didn't give you back your own heart, did she? She kept that for herself."

Sabr strode around to face him and laid her hand upon his breast.

"The heart that beats here is not yours, is it?" she pressed. He would not look at her. "How then can you say," Sabr insisted lowly, "that *she* did not seek to make you hers, exactly as did the Witch?"

Aeriel felt rage surge in her again, dangerously. Not true, not true! She had only wanted to save him, by putting her own living heart in his breast. It had been Talb the Mage who had taken the enchanted darkangel's heart, purged it of the Witch's lead, and placed it into the dying Aeriel's breast.

"I love you," said Sabr.

"Don't say it." The prince's voice was ragged.

Sabr's hand remained upon his heart. She answered, "I don't care whether you can lie with me or not. I only want you to love me in return."

He looked up, then hard away. Aeriel saw the despair in his eyes. "I can't," he whispered to Sabr. "I don't know how. The Witch has got her talons in me still. I can't love you, or *her*, or anyone while the White Witch lives."

The sky seemed to spin over Aeriel. There, he had used it, Sabr's word, that nameless *her*. Sabr reached to cup the prince's face in her hands, but Aeriel hardly saw.

"I'll show you," she told him. "I'll help you." Again he shook his head.

Jealousy consumed Aeriel. How dared the bandit queen? How could Sabr, who had known Irrylath only a few short daymonths, become so close to him? Surely she, Aeriel, had tried every whit as hard to touch him, to lend comfort, to know his heart—only to be repeatedly rebuffed. *You cannot help me*, he had told her once by starlight. *No one can help me*. But she did not hear him say so to Sabr now.

"Whether you love me or not," she told him, "whether you can lie with me or not, I love you. And I only wish that your heart were your own to give as you choose, not some scrap to be tugged to pieces between the teeth of the White Witch and a green-eyed sorceress."

"Oh, cousin," Irrylath told her, "if only that were so."

SICK, SILENTLY RAGING, AERIEL STUM-bled away from camp. The red sand's dry crust broke and crumbled underfoot. She met no one. No one hindered her. The pavilions fell away behind. The night all around stretched dark and still—but she could not escape the hateful words still ringing in her mind, or the memory of what had passed between Irrylath and Sabr.

"Thief!" she gasped, shuddering, scarcely able to draw breath. "Queen of thieves!" Erin had been right. Ducking, Aeriel fought back tears. "Irrylath belongs to *me*."

Something stirred in the darkness ahead of her. Abruptly, Aeriel stumbled to a stop. Hand at her breast, she peered through the pale glimmer of stars and Oceanuslight. Her palm hid the faint glow of the pearl. The creature before her cawed and flexed its wings. As tall as her forearm was long it stood: completely black. Its feathers threw back no sheen at all, depthless as shadow. Aeriel froze. The black bird cawed again and looked at her. In its beak it held a silver pin.

"Greetings, little sorceress," it said, taking the pin in one of its claws to speak.

Aeriel felt her skin prickle. "You are one of the Witch's rhuks."

"Yes," it laughed.

"What do you want of me?" she demanded,

casting about her, wondering how she could have been so blind as to leave the camp alone, unarmed. The empty dunes stretched all around.

"Our lady has a proposition for you," chuckled the rhuk. It played with the silver pin in its toes.

"Do not call her *my* lady," Aeriel spat. "Your mistress was never mine."

"My lady wishes to confer with you," the bird replied. "There is no need for war. Surely this matter can be settled amicably between the two of you, face-to-face."

"I mean to face her," Aeriel returned hotly, "as soon as may be, and with an army at my back."

The black bird hissed. "Relinquish Irrylath. My mistress has a prior claim." It hopped toward her, one-footed, across the sand, its other claw clutching the pin.

"My mistress will reward you with any lover you wish. She will kill Sabr, if you wish."

Aeriel fell back before the Witch's messenger.

"My mistress will make you immortal, like herself, if you so desire," the black bird rasped. "She has always longed for a daughter, an heir...."

"She is not immortal," cried Aeriel, sick with loathing at the sight of the bird: the lorelei made her darkangels' wings from the feathers of such as these. "If she were deathless, she would not fear me."

The rhuk laughed. "Do it for Irrylath's sake," it crooned. "Things will go worse for him if you force my lady to take him from you."

"No!" shouted Aeriel, nearly losing her footing in the soft, treacherous sand.

"Yield!" the bird exclaimed. "Ravenna's luck has deserted you. You don't even know the last stanza of the rime. My mistress is prepared to be generous if you will surrender now."

Aeriel felt the ground sloping sharply upward beneath her feet. The rhuk had backed her against the steep of a dune. For a moment, panic rose in her as she realized she had nowhere left to retreat.

"Your mistress is in mortal terror of me," she answered suddenly, remembering Erin's words. "If the Witch thought she could win, she would have sent her army against us by now."

"My mistress has let your army come this far because it amuses her," the rhuk replied, "to watch children playing at war." The silver pin gleamed in its grasp. "And because you have done her the invaluable service of assembling all her enemies in one place."

Aeriel clenched her teeth. Her hand at her

breast made a fist of the fabric of her gown. How dared this creature corner her and issue its demands? How dared it urge her to surrender Irrylath and the war? As she left the dune and strode toward it, the black rhuk fluttered hastily back, raising a fine, dry rain of sand. Aeriel quickened her stride.

"Why has your mistress sent the likes of you against me?" she inquired evenly. "I have killed your kind before."

"My mistress has no intention of killing you," the black bird hissed, "for then the magic locked in you would escape and be loose in the world. One of her enemies might gather it up, as you did the magic of the starhorse. Better to pin you!"

With a raucous cry, the black bird took wing. For an instant Aeriel thought she had put it to flight. Too late she realized it was flying at her. She felt its wings clap against her face and batted them desperately away. Again it swooped, struck, and this time as she swung and turned, the loose sand shifted beneath her heel, and she fell.

The ground came up hard against her ribs. She felt the black bird's claws upon her back—both sets of talons. It must have dropped the pin, or have it in its mouth again. Gasping, each breath a painful bite, she struggled to raise herself on one elbow and dash the rhuk away. The vile creature clinging to her shoulder made her shake with revulsion.

All at once she felt a stabbing behind her ear, sharp as a little sword. Agony overwhelmed her, too intense even to let her scream. Aeriel rolled and struck wildly at the bird with both hands. To her astonishment, the light of the pearl, no longer hidden, had become a blaze. What had caused it to do so? It had never done so before. The claws of the rhuk abruptly released her. She felt its wings stroke stiffly across her cheek.

"The light, the light!" it crowed.

Dimly, she became aware of the rhuk thrashing on the ground beside her, writhing as though burned. The light of the pearl was already dimming. A horrifying cold had begun to consume her. She groped, putting one hand behind her ear. Her fingers brushed the little knob of silver jutting from the bone. A piercing chill shot through her limbs. She felt as though something were being drawn from her, like the strand yanked from a string of beads. Memory scattered. She thought that she might die of the pain. It was the last thought she had before oblivion blotted out the stars.

———

IT WAS HOURS, MANY HOURS AFTER, that she awakened. Here her memory was very dim, for the pin in her head had stolen her name, working its terrible spell to keep her from knowing herself. The black bird lay dead on the sand beside her. She rose and stood a moment, gazing at it, before wandering away. It had nothing to do with her. She did not remember it. The pearl on her breast glowed faintly, forgotten. She strayed deeper into the desert, forgetting the camp—for that, too, had nothing to do with her now. She had become nobody. A pale, nameless girl.

"And so you wandered, stumbling down into the duaroughs' caves at last, where you felt the pilgrims' Call still broadcasting after all these years, and found your way to me."

Aeriel stirred, hearing the Ancient's voice again. The fiery images had faded from the great glass globe. It hung before her in the air, weightless as gossamer, now showing only a faint azure glow. The room was twilit once more, no longer wholly dark. She gazed at its deep blue walls and hanging gauze. The pallet on which she lay was low and comfortable. Someone held a cool compress to her brow. A strange stiffness prevented her from turning her head. The Ancientlady spoke again.

"Do you know the place to which you and your companions have come?"

Aeriel shifted, trying to sit up. Of course she knew. "The City of Crystalglass."

"Do you know yourself?" the Ancient asked.

That was easy. "Aeriel."

"And do you know who I am?"

Aeriel drew in her breath, realizing for the first time. "Ravenna," she breathed. "The last Ancient of the world."

The one beside her laughed, gently, quietly. "Ravenna is not my name," she replied, "but the name of this city that you call Crystalglass. Its real name is NuRavenna, after a very old city on my own world."

She laughed again, and the airy globe trembled slightly as her words eddied the atmosphere.

"My own name is nearly unpronounceable. That is why, for so long, I was simply called 'the Lady of Ravenna.' Somewhere it was shortened to 'the Lady Ravenna,' and sometimes even 'the Ravenna'—which the duaroughs still use—and finally, now, by the upperlanders, simply 'Ravenna.' You had better go on calling me that. Do you feel well enough to rise?"

Aeriel managed a nod. Her body felt odd—stiff, yet at the same time, strangely supple—

almost as though she had awakened into new flesh never before inhabited or used. The sensation troubled her. For a moment, as she struggled to sit up, the blood ran from her head, and she felt dizzy. Then she steadied. Her hand went to her breastbone, the space there empty now.

"Ravenna," she whispered, "what have you done with my pearl?"

"Hold out your hand," the other answered gently.

As Aeriel did so, the great delicate globe drifted nearer, as if beckoned. Descending, it contracted, solidifying, its blue light deepening, until by the time it touched her palm, it was hard and dense, no bigger than the end of her thumb. Aeriel stared.

"My pearl," she breathed.

"Yes, child," the Ancientlady said. "Though I have made it much more now than a kindled lampwing's egg."

As Aeriel brought it closer to gaze at it, Ravenna's great dusky hand reached past her to touch the glowing jewel. Aeriel felt a little thrill of energy, utterly cool, like a feather's touch, and the light in the tiny corundum globe changed from cerulean to white.

SEVEN

Ravenna's Daughter

AERIEL ROSE FROM THE COUCH. SHE WORE a long, pale, sleeveless gown. Close-woven and weighty, it was no fabric she recognized. Her yellow wedding sari lay at the foot of the pallet, folded in a tiny square. Impulsively, she reached for it and tucked it away in the bodice of her new gown.

The sudden motion of her arm felt novel, unpracticed. The eerie feeling of newness pervaded her still. Aeriel shook herself. Gazing again at the glowing white bead in her hand, she realized now that a tiny chain had been attached to it, a filament of silver so fine she could scarcely see it. It teased across her palm like spider silk.

"What have you done to my pearl?" she asked. "It burns now with a different light."

The Ancient Ravenna stood beside the pallet. She looked drawn, infinitely more weary than she had when Aeriel had last seen her. Her eyes were troubled.

"I have made it a vessel, child, into which I mean to put a treasure of inestimable value. This treasure you must guard for me."

As Ravenna bent near, Aeriel became aware once more of the fragrance of strange, otherworldly flowers that pervaded the lady's robe and hair. The other's dusky, long-fingered hands lifted the pearl from her palm. A moment later, Aeriel felt the fine chain fastened behind the crown of her head, the pearl resting incandescent on her brow.

Its white light suffused her vision like a vapor. Aeriel was conscious all at once of things she had not been able to see before, minute cracks in the glass of the wall across the room, every thread in the lady's garment, a mote of dust upon the other's slipper. And the myriad of tiny lines etching the Ancientlady's face.

With a start, Aeriel perceived for the first time how old Ravenna was. Far from obscuring, the misty light of the pearl seemed to sharpen her view. She felt a subtle welling of new strength. That, too, came from the pearl, she realized.

Softly, Ravenna sighed, and Aeriel was aware of the myriad little air currents which that sigh had set in motion. They went spinning away across the room in eddies faint as featherdown.

"You are to be my envoy, child," the Ancient said and reached as though to pluck something from the air. "This, too, you must bear."

Suddenly in her hands, she clasped a naked sword. Silvery, over three feet in length, it lit the room: a ghostly fire wreathed its blade, stopping just short of the broad crossbar. Aeriel stared. The Ancientlady gestured again, and in her other hand a scabbard appeared, scrolled with interlocking etchings. She sheathed the burning glaive, dousing its flame, and as she did so, Aeriel recognized all at once what it was she held.

"That is the silver pin!" she cried, recoiling, cold horror sweeping over her. Ravenna had changed it somehow—increased its size, made it into a sword. Nevertheless, it could only be the pin, that same sliver of silver with which the Witch's black bird had once pinned Aeriel. Somehow, the pearl imparted this knowledge to her. Ravenna nodded.

"Take it, child. It cannot harm you now."

Aeriel stared at the scabbarded blade in the Ancient's hands. She wanted no part of it. But the other did not withdraw the gift, stood holding it out to her still, patiently, waiting. At last, Aeriel reached and ran her hand along the incised scabbard. She had thought at first it was metal, but touching it, she realized that it was wood. The scrollwork running its length seemed to form a pattern, a figure that she could not quite puzzle out, even with the aid of the pearl.

"Is this weapon for Irrylath?" she whispered. "Am I to take it to him?"

The Ancientlady shook her head. "He has the Edge Adamantine. He does not need another blade."

Through the scabbard, the glaive felt faintly warm. It trembled slightly, like the tremor of a moth's wing, like something alive.

"Is the sword for me, then?" breathed Aeriel.

The Ancient shook her head. "You are but the bearer. No, child. In the end, neither of these gifts is for you."

Reluctantly, Aeriel took hold of the sword's grip. Her hand shook. The blade felt oddly light, seemed to have no weight at all. It balanced in her hand easily as she drew it from the sheath, hummed softly as it pivoted, burning, on the air. She sheathed it, and the sword sang and whispered, ever so softly, a troubling song.

Aeriel set the sword down on the pallet beside her. "To whom am I to give this?"

"Give it to your shadow," Ravenna replied.

Aeriel gazed at her, perplexed. She had no shadow. The temple fire in Orm had burned her shade away. "Lady, I don't understand."

The other smiled ruefully. "Forgive me," she said, "if I speak in rimes, but all will become apparent to you. I promise."

Aeriel fingered the pearl upon her brow. It gleamed, enriching her sight. "Am I to give this up as well?" she asked. "To whom?"

"It is a gift for the world's heir, for my successor—the daughter who must come after me and reign in my stead."

Aeriel stood baffled, helpless to unriddle the other's words. Who was this daughter of whom she spoke? Lightly, Ravenna touched the pearl, and Aeriel felt the touch, strangely magnified, glancing through her like a dart. The pale girl shivered.

"You said you had made my pearl a vessel," she began. "What do you mean for it to hold?"

"Everything," the Ancient said. "All the knowledge of what runs the world, that which I have been gathering these countless years, searching the City's vast libraries and stores before they rot rusting away and spoil into dust."

Her weary features grew serene then, and for a long moment, utterly untroubled.

"The soul of the world must go into that pearl," she continued. "All my sorcery, with which my daughter must heal this sorely beleaguered land, that all will not fall into ruin when I am gone."

"But the Witch," Aeriel protested. "The Witch would undo everything you say! The lorelei is robbing the very life from our land with every drop of water that she steals. A perishing drought rages. She has captured the duaroughs, who work the world's engines belowground, and she has loosed her darkangels upon the kingdoms above...."

Gently, the Ancientlady took her hand and drew her back to sit upon the pallet. "Peace. I know it well. Was it not I that foretold the coming of the Witch?"

Aeriel subsided, sat gazing at the other. Slowly she nodded and felt the dusky lady press her hand. With infinite sadness, Ravenna told her.

"*She* is my daughter, Aeriel. It is to her that you must give the pearl."

"SHE...THE WHITE WITCH IS AN AN-
cient?" Aeriel stumbled, utterly dismayed. All the
world had thought Ravenna the last of the race of
Oceanus. The Ancientlady shook her head.

"No, child. She was born here, on your world."
Abruptly, Ravenna rose. "What do you know of
my people?"

"Little, nothing," Aeriel managed. "In Terrain,
where I was raised, we called you the Unknown-
Nameless Ones."

The Ancientlady gave a short, painful laugh.
"Truly, has our memory crumbled so far?" she
said. Then softly, "Well, perhaps it is a good
thing."

Silence then. The misty light of the pearl made
Aeriel aware of every wrinkle in the coverlet,
every mote in the air, every score upon the scabbard of the burning sword, but nothing the other
said was clear. Reeling, she struggled to collect
herself.

"I know your people came into the world long
ago, from Oceanus. That the land was dead, and
you gave it life. That you made us and all the
herbs and living creatures. That you were like
mothers and fathers to us, and shared your great
wisdom with us, as much as we could understand,

and showed us how to live well and justly, caring for us always...."

Again Ravenna's bitter laugh. "Child, child," she said. "It is not so. We did come from Oceanus long ago, and we did create the living things upon this world. But hardly out of love—for luxury. For our own dalliance. We never shared our knowledge with you. We hoarded it and kept you as ignorant as we could."

The Ancientlady turned suddenly and shook her head, pacing.

"This world was our pleasure garden," the dark lady continued, "and we thought of you, the inhabitants we had fashioned for it, not as our children, but as decorations. Chattels. Slaves."

Coming nearer, she knelt again before Aeriel, speaking urgently. At a sweep of Ravenna's hand, the light in the chamber dimmed. The sword whispered. The pearllight glowed. Once more the colored beads of fire darted, but not upon the surface of the pearl this time. They were within her own mind now, swirling and shimmering, put there by the pearl. With a gasp, Aeriel touched the jewel on her brow and watched the images dancing before her inner eye.

"We are a very old race, Aeriel," the Ancient

said, "immensely learnèd, but far from wise. Once our chariots traveled to the last reaches of heaven. But that was long ago. This moon, your world, was deserted then, dead—until we took it upon ourselves to make it habitable. We created vapors for us to breathe, peoples, animals, plants. Members of our race could spend dozens of hours abroad before needing to return to the Domes. And so from across the heavens we came, to trifle in our garden."

The pearl showed Aeriel everything Ravenna described: the great machinery manufacturing air, the world seeded, the first small creatures released.

"Eventually, the ecology of this world began to evolve on its own. Scientists came then, walking among you and studying your kind. I was such a one. But I dallied, too—to my bitter regret. We all dallied. Countless of your people are our descendants, many generations removed. In my folly, I bore a daughter and raised her here, in NuRavenna, as one of my own race."

A sigh of despair. Aeriel studied the pearl-made image of Ravenna, centuries younger, cradling a fair-skinned infant in her arms. The Ancientlady groaned.

"I should have done what my fellows did with

their own halfling progeny: sent her out into the world to become some great heroine or queen. Instead, selfishly, I kept her, promising that one day she would return home with me. A lie— though one I hoped, desperately, to somehow make true. But that goal proved unattainable. No creature born here can survive on Oceanus. The pull of our world would crush you to bits. Yet I allowed my daughter to believe herself wholly of my Ancient race and that Oceanus was her birthright. Again and again I delayed my return, postponing the inevitable moment when I must reveal to her the truth."

Aeriel saw a young girl barely in womanhood, with the same proud cheeks and high forehead as her mother, her hair the same jet black. Her nose was thinner than Ravenna's, though, the chin more pointed, her complexion paler, the eyes slanted and green.

"Oriencor," Ravenna breathed. "O my daughter, Oriencor."

A space of silence. At last Ravenna roused.

"Then came the news. We had all been recalled. A great disaster upon our home world: war—a thing not known in centuries. Some of my colleagues had prompted wars among you here, upon your world, that they might study them, but that our own world might one day be engulfed in such a conflict, none ever dreamed.

"Most of us sped home at once. My daughter was eager to be off, to join the fight and unleash against those of our own people who had become our foes the Ancient skills which I had taught her. But I demurred. Nor would I allow her to go without me. No one wanted her, anyway: I was the only one who considered her human. At last, I confessed her ancestry to her."

Ravenna's words grew low and halting.

"She went mad. Cursing me, she fled and vanished into the wild marches at desert's edge. When the last chariots departed, I remained behind, searching, but I could find no trace. In the end, in despair, I concluded she must have perished."

In her mind's eye, Aeriel saw the Ancient chariots leaping away on plumes of fire into the black, starry sky. Ravenna's daughter screaming after them as she fled the City. Her mother searching, combing the planet in vain. Aeriel could have wept for the dark-haired halfling girl. When the Ancient spoke again, her tone had flattened into exhaustion.

"Those few of us left upon this world had to decide what to do. Messages from our home world had ceased. Only silence answered our hails. All of our chariots were gone. Some urged the building of new chariots, but we had neither time now nor the means. Already this world had begun to die. Artificial from the first, it had never been intended as self-sustaining. A handful of us, cut off from our mother planet, could never hope to maintain this daughter world as before. We resolved to let it decline gradually and see if we could find a balance-point. We decided to try to salvage the world."

With the aid of the pearl, Aeriel envisioned the world's atmosphere thinning and spinning away into space, whole species of plants and animals dying, people over the generations growing thinner, smaller, hardier.

"And we succeeded," Ravenna said, a trace of animation returning to her voice. "Over the years, we bred new species of vegetation that could survive without our care. We trained the duaroughs to maintain the subterranean machinery that manufactures water and air. Now that the atmosphere had thinned, we could no longer pass outside the Domes without masks to help us breathe. Bit by bit, we withdrew from your people, allowing you to evolve as you would."

The beadwork landscape woven in Aeriel's mind by the pearl became more recognizable, dotted with the herbs and beasts and peoples she knew. Ravenna sighed.

"A point of stasis was reached at last, the entropy halted—or so we thought. Then the Witch appeared, upsetting our delicate equilibrium only subtly at first: wells tainted, dams undermined, cisterns breached. The scarcity of water was always our weakest point. We repaired the damage as best we could. But soon she grew bolder, flaunting her handiwork, spreading drought. As our numbers dwindled, she seized every scrap of technology she could, ransacking the darkened Cities for tools. In time she learned all our most unspeakable arts, with which she means to ravage this world as surely as my race have ravaged Oceanus."

Aeriel gazed at nothing, the images in her mind grown dark.

"And yet," the Ancient whispered, "she is my daughter still."

Aeriel sat in silence, not knowing what to say. "What happened there," she ventured at last, "on Oceanus?"

Ravenna started. An explosion of colors leapt suddenly into Aeriel's thoughts. She shrank from the scenes forming there.

"Plagues," the Ancientlady choked. "Weapons of unimaginable ferocity, horrors unleashed to last a thousand thousand years beyond the lifetimes of their creators and victims alike. Oceanus destroyed itself. That is why it glows in heaven with such a cold and spectral light: quick with the poison that never ends. Nothing is left alive there. *This* is the only world that remains: *this* my daughter's only birthright. If Oriencor would but listen! If I could but persuade her to renounce this mad vengeance, repair the world, and come to NuRavenna to reign after me—"

The Ancient halted, half turned away. Aeriel gazed at her.

"How can I help you, Lady?" she asked finally.

The Ancient turned on her. "Crush the Witch's army," she answered, with such fierceness that Aeriel flinched. "Destroy her darkangels. And lay the pearl of the world in her hand."

Aeriel stared, amazed at what Ravenna seemed to be asking. Was she, Aeriel, to convert the lorelei as once she had rescued a darkangel? But the Witch was infinitely more powerful—and more wicked—than her unfinished darkangel "son" had been. What if Oriencor did not wish to be saved? What if she used the sorcery of the pearl to further her own evil ends?

Yet Ravenna seemed so certain that Aeriel dared not question her. She was an Ancient, after all, with knowledge far superior to Aeriel's own. *I am but the bearer,* the pale girl told herself. *Perhaps it is not necessary that I understand.* The Ancientlady paced, moving restlessly.

"What does the future hold, Aeriel—do you know?"

Aeriel shook her head. Ravenna sighed.

"Nor do I. Many possibilities exist. An infinity: destiny isn't fixed, you know."

Aeriel nodded, trying desperately to comprehend. So Talb the Mage had told her once, many daymonths past. She thought of the Lady Syllva's army, poised on the desert's edge ready to march—or was it already marching by now? How long had she been wandering with the Witch's pin in her head and how long healing here under Ravenna's care? The other returned to her, reaching once more to touch the pearl, and again Aeriel felt the strange, glancing thrill of the Ancientlady's power.

"This jewel on which I have shown you the past," she said, "can also scan ahead in time. I have other such jewels here in the City. And I have sat with them countless hours on end, searching, hoping for a means to undo my daughter's madness."

"What have you seen?" Aeriel asked.

"Many things."

Images stirred once more in the pale girl's mind.

"I have seen your army overthrown and Oriencor triumphant. I have seen Irrylath putting the Blade Adamantine into my daughter's heart. I have seen him killed...."

"No!" Aeriel cried involuntarily, as the scene loomed before her—even though these images of possible futures had a shifting, half-finished look. They were not fixed and vivid as the actual past. Still she recoiled. Ravenna nodded.

"Your husband, yes," she said, "that served my daughter once."

Pain and rage and jealousy swept through Aeriel at the thought of Irrylath. Desperately, she tried to clear her mind, to banish the frightening image that the pearl now wove there: Irrylath falling from the back of the Avarclon, hurtling headfirst through empty air toward a great turbulence below. The vision refused to fade. She shuddered. A tear, hot and salty, spilled down her cheek.

"Say it will not happen," she whispered. "Say that Irrylath will not be killed."

The Ancient, her great, dusky hand so much larger than Aeriel's, brushed the tear from the pale girl's lips.

"I cannot promise you that," she said sadly. "Would that I could. But I have also seen him alive at the end of the war. You killed. You all killed. The possibilities are numberless, and no one is any more likely than another."

She touched the girl's cheek lightly, and Aeriel smelled myrrh. The pearl's horrific speculations vanished now. She sighed in relief.

"That is why I made the rime," Ravenna told her, "to try to guide you and the lons—all of history—toward that one best future I have glimpsed among the rest."

The Ancientlady eyed her very sadly now.

"Have you ever treasured something, child," she asked, "a thing so dear you thought you could never give it up—then learned you must?"

Cold terror returned to Aeriel. No. Never— not Irrylath! She shook her head.

Ravenna sighed. "Soon I must do so—give up what I love best for the good of the world. Come, child. Gird on your sword. The time has come for me to spell you the end of the rime and put my gift into the pearl."

EIGHT

Rime and Shadow

AERIEL'S HEART LEAPT AT THE ANCIENT-
lady's words. Now at last she was to learn the
riddle's end. Almost eagerly, she reached for the
sword that the other had given her. Its strange,
sorcerous feel alarmed her still, but she did as Ravenna bade, belting the long blade's girdle about
her waist. She trusted the dark lady completely.
Ravenna nodded.

"Now say me the rime."

One hand on the swordhilt, the other going to
touch the pearl upon her brow, Aeriel closed her
eyes and began:

"On Avaric's white plain ..."

She recited until she came to the final lines:

> *The Witch of Westernesse's*
> *hag overthrown."*

There she halted. That was all she knew. Without opening her eyes, she sensed the Ancientlady's smile.

"You know most of it, then. Good. Here is the rest:

> *"Whereafter shall commence*
> *such a cruel, sorcerous war,*
> *To wrest recompense*
> *for a land leaguered sore.*

> *With a broadsword bright burning,*
> *a shadow—"*

Abruptly, she broke off. Aeriel blinked in surprise. An image composed of beads of fire had jumped into place upon the near wall of deep blue glass. She recognized the dark features of Ravenna's liege man.

"Lady, a word," he began.

"Melkior," exclaimed the Ancientlady softly. Aeriel sensed her dismay. "I bade that we not be disturbed."

"Forgive me, my liege. The duaroughs insist ..." He halted short, his gaze glancing beyond her to Aeriel. "She's awakened," he murmured in surprise. "You said you would send for me when she revived."

Ravenna's lips compressed, but not with anger. "Time presses," she began.

The dark man's eyes widened suddenly. "And you've given her the sword? You swore that you would not, not until—"

She shook her head. "I thought to spare you."

"No!" Melkior cried. "Lady, hold off. Hold off until I come!"

His image vanished. Ravenna whirled. "Haste, child," she said urgently. "I had hoped to accomplish this while Melkior was yet occupied with your companions, but he will be here in another moment. Quickly—draw the sword."

Aeriel stared at the Ancientlady. "Am I to defend you against your liege man?" she stammered.

The dusky lady hurriedly shook her head. "No. I would not ask that of you. Nor would I wish any harm to come to Melkior. But we must lose no time. Unsheathe the glaive."

Aeriel did so. The blade leapt from the scabbard almost without her will. The misty fire along it burned and whispered.

"Hold it up before you," Ravenna bade.

Aeriel held the glaive point-upward, clasping its

long hilt in both hands. It seemed to have no weight, stood humming upon the air. Lightly, deliberately, the Ancientlady brought her palm down upon the point. Aeriel started, feeling a jolt of energy course through the blade. The pearl upon her brow blazed, and for a moment, the white fire running along the sword flared in a wreath of burning colors.

"Sheathe it," Ravenna said.

Aeriel slid the blade, white-lit again, into its case. The light of the pearl on her brow had diminished now. Holding her hand, the Ancientlady seemed suddenly short of breath.

"Don't fear," she said.

Carefully, she cupped her palm to the pale girl's forehead. Aeriel felt a sudden rushing, as of hurtling headlong, or as of some unbreakable thread spinning out of Ravenna and into the pearl. Its force held Aeriel transfixed. She could not have moved if she had wished. Only snatches reached her mind—of strange magics, indescribable sorceries, the woven patterns for all living things— all winding themselves away, unreadable, in the jewel's depths. Already the thread had begun to dwindle and slacken. Aeriel felt a change of air as, all at once, the wall behind Ravenna parted, and her liege man dashed through.

"Stop!" he cried. "Lady, stop—"

Gently, the Ancient took her palm from the pale girl's brow. "Peace, Melkior," she whispered, turning. "It's done."

Her voice was hollow, her face gone ashen beneath the dusky color of her skin. The dark man started forward with a cry, and the Ancientlady sagged into his arms. Aeriel bit back a gasp as she watched Ravenna's liege man support her to the black glass floor. The Ancientlady was dying; Aeriel realized it in horror. The pearl, blazing now, enabled her to feel some echo, as beneath her own breastbone, of the other's heart, now guttering like a spent lamp's flame.

"Lady—Lady, what have you done?" she cried, falling to her knees beside her and Melkior.

Ravenna lay supine in the dark man's arms. She gazed at Aeriel. Softly, with great effort, she spoke.

"Child, have you not understood . . . a word I have said? All myself—all that I have gathered— I have placed into that jewel. You must bear it to the world's heir . . . to my daughter. Destroy Oriencor's army," Ravenna breathed, "and put the pearl into her hand."

A grimace swept over the Ancient's face. Melkior's grip upon her tightened. "No, Lady," he implored her. "Don't leave me."

Wearily, she turned to him, touching his cheek. "Had I another choice...but we both know I must."

Her eyes drifted closed. Her hand upon the other's cheek slid to the floor. No breath now stirred the Ancientlady's breast: no pulse moved in her veins. *Ravenna is dead,* thought Aeriel, stunned. *How can that be?* She shook her head, her thoughts disjointed. *Soon she will be turning into ash.* Then, *No, the Ancients' bodies do not crumble at death. They remain perfectly preserved, forever, unless they are burned.* For a long moment, Melkior simply stared at his lady's still form; then he buried his face in her hair.

Behind him, standing in the open doorway, Aeriel caught sight of the three duaroughs: Maruha, Collum, and Brandl. The duarough woman looked as fit as the other two now, well recovered from her wound. The three of them hung back, as if in reverence turned to dismay. Maruha's face was wide-eyed, Collum's ashen and grim. Brandl looked as though he, too, might weep.

Shaking, Aeriel rose. The pearl upon her brow burned heatless white. In its depths, the Ancient's sorceries moved, unreachable: incomprehensible to her even if she could have found and read them. *How am I to complete my task?* she thought numbly. *How am I to defeat the Witch and convert her to her mother's cause?* The sword at her side murmured softly, sang. The only other sound in the room was the dark man's sobbing. A hand slipped into Aeriel's. Someone was tugging at her. Looking down, she saw Maruha.

"Come," the duarough woman said softly. "Come, Sorceress—Lady Aeriel. We must be off. We should not stay."

AERIEL STOOD UPON THE RED DESERT sands. The smoked glass of the Dome rose at her back, curving inward over the City, now left behind. The airlock had proved a series of hatched doorways, which the duaroughs opened readily by complicated and unfathomable means. Yet, watching by pearllight, Aeriel felt a whisper of comprehension steal eerily over her: some aftereffect of Ravenna's sorcery, perhaps. She almost believed that if she had put her mind to it, she could have opened the Ancient doors herself.

Instead, she turned heavily away. Thoughts of the dying Ravenna chilled her still. Memory of the Ancient interrupted by her liege man filled Aeriel with bitterness—only a few more moments, and she might have known the whole of the rime! Her back to the Dome, Aeriel stood gazing out at the desert dunes. It was nightshade, and by the tilt of the stars, not many hours after Solstarset.

"But it was nightshade when we came," she murmured and shook her head, amazed. Almost a daymonth spent in NuRavenna—and how many more wandering the desert and the caves? Irrylath's army must be halfway to the Waste by now! So much time lost...Maruha beside her nodded.

"We've been within for hours upon hours, Lady—handfuls of dozens of them—while you and the holy Ancient conferred."

Aeriel glanced at the duaroughs. *They think I have the rime,* she thought. *They think the Ancient-lady gave me all of it—that I am prepared to meet the Witch.*

"We spent the time going about under the Dome, Sorceress," Brandl added as he and Collum wrestled with the airlock's final closure, "surveying the City's machines—for Lord Melkior said we must be gone in haste as soon as his lady had given you all you needed if we were to join this war in time."

His young face was shining with expectancy, his words eager and bold. Already he seemed to have forgotten Ravenna fallen, Ravenna dying. *But I don't have all I need,* Aeriel wanted to scream. *She only gave me half the rime's end—not enough! Not nearly enough. I don't even know what the pearl is, or the sword.* To calm herself, she took a deep breath. The outside air felt deliciously thin and cool.

"You must not call me 'lady' or 'sorceress,'" she answered distantly instead. "I'm neither."

Collum snorted. "Indeed! And I suppose you have no pearl upon your brow, Lady, nor a sword that sings ever so softly in gift from the Ravenna herself."

"Who is gone now," whispered Aeriel, touching the swordhilt, then the pearl. She felt lost. "Ravenna is dead."

"You're her heir," Maruha insisted.

Aeriel shook her head. *Not I,* she thought. *The Ancient boons are not for me.* Yet a desperate resolve had begun to fill her. No matter that she had not the last of the rime. No matter that she now bore two strange sorcerous gifts the purpose of which she did not even know. Somehow, by means she did not yet understand, she must persuade Ravenna's daughter to renounce her treachery and become the world's heir.

"Oh, please, Sorceress," Brandl cried, coming

forward. His hand had gone to his little harp. "Will you tell me the rest of the rime? I'll sing it wherever I go." He threw a glance—nervous and defiant by turns—in Maruha's direction. "I mean to be a bard, whatever my aunt may say."

"Sooth—my whole family, worthless!" the duarough woman muttered. "You're as bad as your fool uncle, lad." But she made no move to interfere.

Numbly, Aeriel knelt before him on the cool sand. "I cannot give you all," she said. "For Ravenna did not give me all. But I will give you what I can:

"Whereafter shall commence
such a cruel, sorcerous war,
To wrest recompense
for a land leaguered sore.

With a broadsword bright burning,
a shadow ..."

Aeriel bit her tongue and fell silent. She did not know the rest. She could not bear to look at Brandl's face, to see the disappointment she knew must be there when he realized how pitifully little she had gained for all her time in Ravenna's care. Dismay swept over Aeriel as she allowed herself to consider: so many futures possible. How could they hope to win this war without the rime's end as a guide...?

She had no time to think more—aware suddenly that even though her words had ceased, the recitation of the rime had not. Another voice now whispered it, a soft, strange voice that creaked like oiled wood. Aeriel's startled gaze went to the sword at her side—but it was not the sword that spoke. It was the scabbard.

> *"With a broadsword bright burning,*
> *a shadow black as night*
> *From exile returning*
> *shall champion the fight...."*

The scrolls upon the inlaid surface of the wood swirled and shimmered, shifting their pattern, becoming a bird.

> *"For love of one above who, flag unfurled,*
> *lone must stand,*
> *The pearl of the soul of the world*
> *in her hand...."*

The bird stretched, long narrow wings coming free of the sheath. Its white feathers shimmered.

"When Winterock to water
  falls flooding, foes to drown,
Ravenna's own daughter
  shall kindle the crown."

Aeriel stared at the slim white bird upon the swordcase. Its bright, round eye stared back at her. She felt a rush of wild joy and disbelief.

"Heron!" she cried.

Maruha and Collum both stood gaping. Brandl hastily fell back. The heron blinked slowly, her metamorphosis only half complete.

"By rights," she replied woodenly, "in my present form, you should be calling me Scabbird, but I suppose 'heron' will do if it must. Now let be. This is a difficult transformation."

The white bird's long, sharp bill snicked shut. She closed her eye and, flapping mightily, struggled free of the sheath. She gained size as she did so, her feathers losing their silvery gleam, till she stood on the desert sand at last, ruffling her snowy pinions and flexing her long, ungainly legs.

"What magery is this?" Maruha whispered.

"Ravenna's messenger-bird," Aeriel laughed, reaching to stroke the other's white breast feathers, "that I have not seen since Orm."

The heron ruffled and danced away. "I have

been about my lady's business," she snapped, "as you had all best be."

Aeriel nodded. She felt buoyed up. She had the rime now! As well as the pearl, and the sword—none of them riddled out as yet, but all of them in her hand. Turning back to the dua-roughs, she said, "Tell me, Brandl, have you got the verse?"

The young bard goggled a moment, still gazing at the bird—but then he regained himself and said all three long stanzas of the rime back to her, even the last, almost perfectly on the first try. She nod-ded, smiling. Perhaps he would make a bard after all, despite Maruha. He had a bard's memory, at least.

"Well, Lady Sorceress," Maruha said at last. "We had best be on our way. The Ancientlord Melkior told us of underpaths not far from here. We must return to our people and tell them all we have learned of our fellows forced to serve the Witch."

"We must march belowground to rescue them!" Brandl added, face flushed with excitement, his eyes bright.

"He's not an Ancient," Collum muttered be-neath his breath. "Lord Melkior's a halfling, like the Witch."

"No longer," answered Brandl sobering suddenly. "He's a golam now, all gears and wire—like the starhorse." His voice dropped softer still. "The Ravenna rebuilt him after Oriencor's treachery left him for dead, a thousand years ago. He has served the Ancientlady since."

Maruha hissed at him, impatient to be gone. "We're off," she said, offering her hand to Aeriel in the duaroughish fashion, but Aeriel would not take it. Such a gesture was too formal by far. A sorrow almost as strong as her joy at meeting the heron stole over her now. Kneeling, she embraced the duarough woman.

"Fare well. I am in your debt."

"Debt?" Maruha exclaimed. "Sooth—nonsense, Lady. The removing of the pin was the Ravenna's doing, and if you had not kept the weaselhounds from us, we should all have gone to the Witch."

Brandl, having seemingly conquered his astonishment at last, stood studying the heron intently as she pouted and fluttered in the amber sand, ignoring him. Maruha seized her nephew's arm.

"I'll make a song of you, Lady Sorceress!" he called as his aunt pulled him purposefully away. Only Collum remained, shifting uneasily from foot to foot.

"The luck of all the ways go with you, Lady," he murmured at last.

"And with you, Collum," Aeriel said.

"If you fail," he started, stopped, then charged ahead. "If you fail us, Lady, we are all lost. No Ravenna remains to save us now."

Abruptly Collum turned and strode after the others. Aeriel watched them heading for a low outcropping of rock jutting up from the sand not many paces distant. For a moment, Aeriel's heart grew cold as she considered the truth of Collum's words. All rested upon her now. And on the pearl and the sword and the rime. Rising, she brushed the desert from her knees. The heron returned to stand beside her, shaking the red grit out of her feathers. Reaching the outcropping, the three duaroughs waved. Aeriel raised her own hand in farewell as they disappeared from view.

AERIEL TURNED FROM THE DISTANT rocks and rested one hand against the City's dark glass Dome. She chafed her arms against the cool breeze and shivered, feeling alone suddenly, despite the heron. Absently, she ran her fingers through the downy feathers cresting the white bird's hard little skull. The heron tolerated her touch with indifference.

"Do you know the meaning of the rime?" she asked.

"I only carry my lady's messages," the bird replied. "I do not interpret them."

Aeriel sighed, eyeing a little amber scorpion traveling across the sand. The heron darted after it, stabbing in its wake. "Hark," she observed, through a billfull of sand. "Your shadow nears."

Aeriel frowned, not understanding. She fingered the sword pommel a moment, remembering Ravenna's words—but she had no shadow, had had none since Orm. No shade now trailed her by any light. Sighing in frustration, she let her eyes stray to the far horizon. The Witch's Mere lay directly ahead. She understood this somehow without having to think about it. The downy light of the pearl pervaded her senses.

Then something stirred among the shadows of the dunes, something dark as a Shadow itself, black as the night. Aeriel beheld a figure coming toward her across the swells of sand. Even so distant and by starlight, she recognized it at once: that which, like a second self, had shadowed her since desert's edge, the one she had dreaded and fled so desperately—because to have turned and faced her follower would have reminded her intolerably of her own identity and of all the other memories that the pin had banned. She felt no fear now as the dark form approached.

"So you have found me at last," the pale girl said. "I'm glad."

"You led me a merry chase," the other snapped. "When I had no light to track you belowground, I thought you lost—until the heron found me."

Aeriel gazed at the one halted before her. Erin stood as tall as she herself did now. The dark girl wore a blue shift, sleeveless with great open armholes for ventilation. If she had carried a desert walking stick, Aeriel might almost have taken her for one of the Ma'a-mbai. Barefoot and sandy, the dark islander looked weathered thin, her skin still black as a starless sky. Erin cast a reproachful glance at the white bird.

"She led me within sight of the City's beacon before abandoning me, hours since."

The heron fluffed. "And why should I do more?" she inquired. "You are a demanding shadow."

Having lost her scorpion in the sand, she stalked haughtily away.

"Are you well?" Aeriel asked.

Erin reached to touch her hand, as if to assure herself the other was real. She nodded. "And you? You look strange somehow—unweathered. The heron told me what befell you, of the black bird and the pin."

Aeriel shook off the odd, lingering feeling of newness and drew the dark girl near. "Yes, I am well," she said. "Ravenna tended me." When Erin released her at last, she continued, "But I have had no news of Irrylath and the army in daymonths."

The dark girl shook her head, laughing a little with fatigue and relief. "Nor I, since I left them two daymonths ago."

Aeriel touched the other's cheek, remembering the distant bustle of the camp and the sigh of tents. Two daymonths—had it really been so long? "Tell me what happened when first you discovered me gone."

Erin leaned wearily against the Dome. "A furious uproar and a fruitless search ensued. Of course your disappearance was all *my* fault—so your husband would have it, as I was the last who had been with you." The dark girl's voice grew guarded, tight. "At last a sentry confessed to having glimpsed you striding off across the dunes, and your fine prince Irrylath almost ran him through."

Listening, Aeriel closed her eyes. The pearl strung all Erin described before her mind's eye in moving beads of fire.

"Your tracks beyond camp's edge were found at last, ending in a moldering scatter of stinking feathers. Irrylath grew wild at the sight of them, choking out something about the lorelei building the wings of her darkangels from such."

A dozen paces away from them, the heron preened. The stars above burned bright and cold, little pinpricks of light. Aeriel eyed the constellation called the Maidens' Dance.

"And then?"

"When it was concluded you must have been plucked away by icari, taken hostage by the Witch, the camp fell into turmoil."

Aeriel flinched, her mind on fire with the other's words.

"What of Irrylath?" she insisted. Every news of him was precious to her.

Erin's voice grew tighter still. "Great protestations of grief! He should have appointed you bodyguards; he should have warned you against walking unescorted abroad—small help all this contrition after the fact," she scoffed. "His mother the Lady Syllva spoke of taking the Edge Adamantine away from him lest he do himself or others harm."

The pale girl bowed her head, appalled. "And

when you departed to follow, to find me," she managed, "was he yet wild with this grief?"

Said Erin acidly, "His cousin Sabr comforted him."

White jealousy flared in Aeriel then, hot as a flame. She felt the dark girl's hand tighten upon her own.

Erin muttered, "I'll put a dagger in his heart when next I see him."

"You'll not," Aeriel exclaimed, her eyes flying open now. Erin tried to pull away, but the pale girl held her. "He's mine. If you love me, you'll leave him to me."

Erin said nothing for a long moment. At last she asked, "So you do love him still—even now?"

Aeriel sighed and could not answer. What she felt was rage and pain and longing—a fierce, unquenched longing for Irrylath's love. The dark girl looked at her.

"*I* love you," she said, very softly. "Freely. And always will."

Aeriel reached to touch her cheek, but Erin turned away, crossing her arms. The pale girl eyed her a few moments silently, before murmuring, "So you alone did not believe I had been taken by icari."

The other shook her head. "No. I saw the dark-angel in Pirs scream and flee at the sight of you."

"Did you tell Irrylath this?"

Erin snorted. "Your husband does not listen to me."

Aeriel looked down, deeply grieved for Erin's suffering on her account. Irrylath's, too. She had never meant to cause either of them pain. Aeriel lifted her gaze toward the distant, unseen Witch's Mere. The soft white glow of the pearl filled her eyes.

"So you set out on your own in search of me."

"If Ravenna's heron had not found me a day-month past, I should be searching still," Erin answered, calmer now. "What will you do with Irrylath when you return?"

Aeriel sighed and shook her head. The wind from the desert was cool and full of fine sand that polished at her anklebones. The heron, testing her wings, rose into the air, hovering a moment before realighting. Aeriel looked away.

"I am not returning with you, Erin."

The dark girl pivoted to stare at her. Abruptly, she shoved away from the Dome and halted a few paces from Aeriel. "What do you mean?" she demanded. "You must ride at the head of the army that has gathered in your name! I did not travel all this way to be told you will not go back."

Carefully, Aeriel unbuckled the sword at her hip. "Ravenna has given me another task. I mean to meet the Witch, but not in battle. I must confront her face-to-face."

"Are you mad?" Erin cried, catching her arm.

"Bear word back," Aeriel told her, "of our allies the duaroughs marching underland against the Witch. Say that I have spoken with the Ancient Ravenna."

"No!" Erin exclaimed. "I won't. I'll not leave you." She did not let go of the pale girl's arm. "If you mean to face the Witch unguarded, I'll stand at your side."

Aeriel shook her head and held out the sword. A little of the Ancient rime was slowly becoming clear to her. The glaive burned and whispered in its sheath. "Someone must champion the fight in my stead," she said softly. "Whom can I trust but you?"

Erin looked at the sword, then back at Aeriel. The pale girl waited. At last, very reluctantly, Erin took the sword. "Oh," she cried, gripping the pommel and sheath. "Oh, what is this? It feels *alive*."

Aeriel did not answer—for truly, she did not yet know what power the sword might hold. The Witch's pin was what it once had been. What manner of thing into which Ravenna had now transformed it, she could not say. Intently, the dark girl girded it about her waist. The sword hung, shimmering in its sheath. As Erin lifted the now-plain scabbard to study the silvery grain of the wood, running one finger along its sheath's smooth edge, Aeriel felt a strange sensation, as of something lightly stroking her side. She shivered, frowning, and brushed herself. When Erin warily tried to pull the blade free, it would not come.

"Soft," Aeriel murmured, sure only as she spoke that what she said was so. "Now is not the time, though you will be able to draw it at need." The pearl told her this, she realized, scarcely stopping to wonder at it. She gazed out over the dry, crested dunes before turning back to Erin. "Fare you well," she said.

"Wait—" the dark girl began, groping for words, unwilling still to let her go. "Have you no journey fare, no water?"

For the first time Aeriel noticed the little sack of provisions and the waterskin slung from the other's shoulders. The pale girl shook her head. She felt not the slightest hunger or thirst.

"The pearl feeds me," she answered, certain suddenly that she would need no nourishment so long as she wore Ravenna's jewel upon her brow. As Erin embraced her, Aeriel pulled the wedding sari from her bodice and handed it to her. "Give this to Irrylath," she said, "to make a banner of. And tell my husband he will find me at the Witch's Mere."

The dark girl carefully tucked the folded square of yellow silk into her shift. Aeriel drew back. Behind them, the City's bright beacon flared suddenly from the highest tower within the Dome. Aeriel started, turning.

"Heron, what is it?" she cried.

The white bird skimmed to her across the dunes. "Melkior is burning my lady to ash," she said. "Time we all of us were gone."

She veered away then, but Aeriel reached to catch her wing.

"Wait, heron. Where are you bound?"

The Ancient's messenger indignantly shook herself free.

"I have my own part still in Ravenna's task" was all she would say before gliding away across the crests of sand. The desert air lifted her up, soaring. Within the Dome, the beacon fire blazed higher, brighter still. Aeriel and Erin watched the white bird dwindle in the distance and disappear.

The dark girl shouldered her pack and water bag and embraced Aeriel again. At last she lifted her hand in farewell as she started away. Aeriel raised her own in reply before the other disappeared among the dunes. A moment later, she herself strode off in another direction across the sand.

NINE

Bright Burning

AERIEL TRAVELED ALONE OVER THE END-
less dry dunes toward the Witch's Mere. The pearl
helped her see soft places in the sand, avoid those
banks that had begun to shift. She walked a long
time before pausing to rest, and even then it was
not fatigue that stopped her. *If I press on too hard,
Erin will do the same,* she found herself thinking,
illogically, and yet she halted, strangely sure it was
for Erin's sake.

She envisioned the dark girl, miles away, sinking down, one hand resting on the pommel of the
sword, unwilling to unfasten it, even now. When
Erin brought her little skin water bag to her lips,
Aeriel tasted water. The dark girl took a handful
of flavorless chickseed from her pouch and chewed
on it, coughed dryly, sipped again. She sighed

heavily and at last lay down, cheek pillowed on her arm.

Shoulders slumping, Aeriel felt a kind of resonant fatigue. Abruptly, she caught herself, surprised how vivid her imagining had been. It was not her own weariness she sensed, but that of her far-off friend. Did some connection now link them: pearl to sword? Aeriel frowned, wondering. The dark girl's presence seemed to overlie her own vision—lightly, yet as distinctly as an image reflected on water. If she ignored it, it faded. Yet when she paid it heed, it sharpened, growing more vivid. Exhausted, Erin slept. Later, when she awoke, Aeriel rose and walked on.

The night lengthened. At last Aeriel neared the desert's edge. The sand underfoot turned from pale orange to greyer drab. Bits of parched, broken ground showed through. An occasional frayed shoot thrust up through a crack. She sensed Erin, leagues distant, also nearing the desert's edge. The dark girl hove into sight of the allied camp sooner than Aeriel had expected. The terrain of the Waste was uneven there, fraught with canyons and cliffs. Guards and sentries stood posted everywhere. They stared at Erin as though she had returned from the dead.

"You know me," she snapped wearily. "Stop gaping." They made no attempt to stop her, only called for their captains. "Where is he, Irrylath?" Erin demanded. "I bring word of Aeriel."

They stared at the glaive, burning white in its sheath. "The Aeriel!" she heard others murmuring, abuzz. "A message from the Aeriel . . ."

Far away, the pale girl had to smile. Already her name, like Ravenna's, was being used as a title. Impatient, Erin strode past the sentries without waiting for their leave. She headed toward the great council tent at the center of the camp. Rose silk, it billowed huge, breathing and sighing in the slight desert wind. Again, the sentries gaped, but these had the presence of mind to cross their pikes. Erin halted. Aeriel heard voices through the tent's open entryway.

"My son, we must press on. . . ."

"Brother, Aeriel or no Aeriel, our troops cannot simply continue to languish here."

". . . nightshade upon daymonth, Cousin, going nowhere—"

Hand resting on the pommel of her sword, Erin told the sentries, "Let me pass. I come from Aeriel."

Within, the drone of discussion abruptly ceased.

"Who's there?" demanded a voice. Though rough, it was surely Irrylath's. Aeriel fought the leaping of her heart.

"Sentry, answer your commander," a second voice directed, lighter pitched, but for all that, more like the prince's than Aeriel had ever realized: his cousin, Sabr.

Aeriel's throat knotted, and a bitterness welled in her mouth. She had not wanted to think of the bandit queen again so soon. Other voices murmured. At Irrylath's word, the two guards uncrossed their spears and stood aside. Erin entered. Through the dark girl's eyes, Aeriel glimpsed the Lady Syllva and her Istern sons, her own brother Roshka and Talb the Mage—even the lyon Pendarlon.

They clustered about a folding camp table on which rested a map weighted with odd objects: a sheathed dagger, a flagon, a stone. Someone moved through the others from the table's far side. Walking the Wasteland, absorbed in her vision, Aeriel stumbled. Dismay glanced through her. She scarcely recognized the man. She felt Erin's start of surprise echo her own.

"Oh, husband," Aeriel murmured. "Irrylath."

He was so thin, he looked weathered to the

bone. The broad, high planes of his cheeks stuck sharply out, the cheek beneath hollow and shadowed. His sark hung loose from the shoulders, the sash at the waist cinched tight. He looked like a whippet, like a desert racing cat, like a man in whom some guilty inner fire burned, consuming him.

"He won't live to reach the Witch's Mere!" Aeriel found herself whispering in terror, and the image came to her again, unbidden, of Irrylath falling toward storm-tossed emptiness. Desperately, she thrust the fearful thought away. She stood halted in the middle of the flat, grey expanse of Wasteland now, staring at nothing, seeing only what was happening in Syllva's camp leagues upon leagues away, watching through Erin's eyes.

"You are much changed, Prince," the dark girl said. A gap of several paces separated them.

"And you," the one before her answered, "late companion to my wife, you who deserted us so abruptly—in secret, so soon after she was taken—that many wondered what your part in her abduction might have been." His words were quiet, keen and hard. "I, too, had a trusted companion once," the prince continued, "one who betrayed me to the Witch."

Miles distant, Aeriel flinched at the barely veiled accusation. Before him, Erin snorted, refusing to be baited.

"I left because my errand was urgent," she snapped. "Now I have returned, having lately been with Aeriel."

The others in the tent stirred, murmuring. Syllva, the Lady of Isternes, took a step forward as though to speak, but her son the prince of Avaric spoke first.

"Have you?" he scoffed. "Then you have been to the Witch's palace and back." His voice held such a brittle edge that Aeriel shuddered.

"I have been to the City of Crystalglass," the dark girl replied, her own voice angry but controlled. The prince's very presence grated on her. Aeriel had never before this moment realized the extent of their antipathy. "*That* is where Aeriel had gone."

"You lie!" His vehemence surprised even Erin. "Either way, you lie! If you have been to the City, you have not been with Aeriel. If you have been with her and are now returned, you belong to the Witch."

Irrylath's brothers shifted, shaking their heads. Hadin, the youngest, murmured, "Brother, hold...."

But Irrylath ignored them all, his eyes locked on Erin's.

"I have been with Aeriel," the dark girl told him quietly, firmly, "at Crystalglass—"

"And is she well?" the prince exclaimed, almost calm again suddenly. "Then tell me what the Witch had made of her: is it a lorelei like herself that devours men's souls—or perhaps a female darkangel, an icarë? She needs another to replace me, you know. She's only got six now. Or a harridan, perchance, such as we met at Orm—or even a wraith? Is that it? Has she made my wife into a wraith? Tell me."

Aeriel stood, fists doubled at her breasts, able to perceive it all so vividly across the miles, yet powerless to intervene. Rather than stand helpless, she almost wished that she could break the link between the dark girl and herself: tear the pearl from her own brow, or the sword from Erin's hand. But she dared not lose sight of Irrylath, even for a moment.

"She was well when last we spoke, earlier this fortnight," Erin replied, outwardly implacable now. Yet Aeriel felt how hot the dark girl's anger burned just beneath the skin.

"Then why has she not returned with you?" Irrylath's cry was not so wild this time, but full of anguish and a fury to match and overmatch the dark girl's ire. Aeriel stood dismayed.

"She is on her way to face the Witch," Erin replied evenly.

"Alone?" The prince of Avaric shook his head. A weak, unsteady laugh escaped his lips. One hand was in his hair now, clenched, become a fist. He whispered, "Lies."

"Irrylath, Irrylath, calm yourself," Aeriel exclaimed.

No one heard—but her words were echoed by the Lady Syllva. Pendarlon rumbled. Roshka spoke low and urgently to Hadin beside him. Talb the Mage shifted uneasily, fingering his beard. Unheeding, Irrylath touched the hilt of the Edge Adamantine, much as Erin's hand rested upon the broadsword Bright Burning. Aeriel felt the dark girl's jaw hardening.

"I am not a liar, Prince Irrylath."

Her hand tightened on the sword. With a start, the young man leaned forward suddenly, staring at Erin's weapon. Aeriel heard the sharp intake of his breath. His eyes had become like blue lampflames burning.

"That glaive you bear is Witch-made," he breathed. "I doubt it not. Her handiwork is unmistakable—"

"*Aeriel* gave me this," Erin grated. "Disbelieve if you dare, you faithless wretch!" She spat the last word. "It is only your own falsehood gnawing at you. That and the knowledge that this whole war hangs on *her*, and you are nothing beside her. No match to her and never will be ..."

Hoarse as a madman, the young man cried, "You are some catspaw of the Witch!"

Without warning, he sprang, covering the paces between himself and Erin in less than a moment. The dark girl's eyes widened. Through her, Aeriel saw the sweat on Irrylath's brow, the scars threading one cheek, the animosity in his hot blue eyes.

"My son, no!" the Lady Syllva gasped.

Adamantine flashed in the prince's hand: its snaking blade gleamed with a white radiance, its edge so keen it could cut anything. Already Pendarlon was springing. Behind him, Roshka and the prince's brothers shouted, bolting forward to stay him. The guards in the entryway were nearer— but they would all be too late. The sword was beginning to fall. It would be over between one heartbeat and the next. Perceived through the dark girl's eyes, Irrylath's blade almost appeared to Aeriel to be flashing down upon herself. Seething, the dark islander stood, refusing to retreat.

"Erin!" Aeriel screamed, throwing up one arm

as though somehow to fend off the adamantine blade.

In that same instant, Erin unsheathed the sword. She brought her own long, straight, burning blade up in a clean arc to meet the white serpentine edge of the prince's shortsword. The two blades met with a sound at once like a silver bell and a low flute note and a bandolyn string sharply plucked. Aeriel fell to her knees, feeling the shock resonate along her whole length as the Edge Adamantine was blocked and held. The blade that could cut anything could not cut the burning sword.

IRRYLATH CRIED OUT. GRIMACING, HE clutched his wrist as though he meant to release his weapon or lift it away, but it seemed he could not move. The white fire that swirled about the dark girl's blade threaded upward along Adamantine to touch the prince's hand. With a groan, he sank to his knees. Erin stood gazing at him, astonished.

"Let be!" Aeriel cried out. "Have done!"

And this time, somehow, the others in the tent leagues distant heard. The Lady Syllva halted where she stood. Roshka and Irrylath's brothers broke off their headlong rush. Pendarlon checked, snarling. The guards dashing in from the doorway froze. As Erin lifted Bright Burning away from Irrylath's blade, the fire touching his hand vanished, and the prince slumped, sword arm falling heavily to the ground. Adamantine made a clean, dustless cut in the earth. Sabr ran to him, her own dagger drawn. Erin ignored her, holding the glaive upright before her, staring at it.

"I did not mean to draw this blade," the dark girl whispered. "Something seemed to steer my hand. I meant only to stand defiant until the last moment, to see if you truly meant to have my life." Still staring at the blade, she was speaking to the prince. "I thought no need for swords. I thought the others would stop you."

The broadsword sang and hummed. Aeriel heard her own sobbing in the sound. Panting, Irrylath cradled his arm as though it were painful—or numb. A stab of fear went through Aeriel. She had no idea whether the sword's fire had harmed him permanently. He seemed dazed. All the others in the tent were casting about with baffled or frightened looks, save Pendarlon, who, staring at Erin's blade, was making a low catgrowl.

"Stop, stop," Aeriel wept, hardly realizing that she spoke aloud.

Now everyone was staring at the glaive, even Irrylath. Sabr steadied his head, which lolled as though he might swoon. Through Erin, Aeriel watched the sword begin to flicker and waver, like a long white flame. The misty candescence and the blade itself merged until the whole sword was a tongue of fire. Aeriel staggered to her feet. The flame also rose, elongating, narrowing. Through the dark girl's astonished eyes, she saw the flame taking on a human shape. With a start, Aeriel recognized herself, then felt her own being drawn irresistibly across the miles until it merged into the flame. Turning to her husband, she called his name.

"Irrylath," she said urgently. "Irrylath, heed me. You are not mistaken. Erin's sword *was* Witch-made once, but Ravenna has changed it to serve our cause."

The prince of Avaric shook his head, gazing at her in disbelief. Aeriel saw Sabr's hands upon him tighten.

"Pay no heed, Cousin," she murmured. "That is some image of the Witch. The shadowmaid is in league with your tormentor. She was never your friend."

Irrylath seemed not to hear her, his attention fixed on the image in the sword. Aeriel choked down her sudden fury at the intervention of Sabr. An outburst of jealousy now would serve neither herself nor Irrylath. Resolutely, she ignored the bandit queen, spoke only to the prince.

"Husband, it is I."

"You can't be," Irrylath cried out hoarsely. "The Witch sent her darkangels to steal you away."

Aeriel shook her head. "Not so. One of her black birds set a pin behind my ear."

"I would have told you that if you had let me," Erin growled between her teeth. She pulled the folded sari from her shift and tossed it down before the prince who, with a gasp, touched the cascade of yellow silk about his knees. Lifting his eyes, he gazed at the sword, as a man dying of thirst might gaze upon a mirage of water.

"Oh, Aeriel," Irrylath whispered. "If only it were you...."

"It isn't," Sabr hissed desperately. "An image! Some clever trap."

Aeriel felt the pearl upon her brow gleaming coolly. An idea formed itself in her mind.

"The rime," she said. "I have the last of Ravenna's riddle now. Will that convince you?" She raised her eyes and voice to the others in the tent. "Will that convince you all?"

Irrylath struggled to his feet, throwing off Sabr's persistent hands. His voice rang clear and certain suddenly. "Speak it," he cried. "Say the rime, and if you are truly Aeriel, unharmed and not in the Witch's power, I will know you."

His one hand was clenched about their wedding silk. The other, his sword hand, twitched as though trying to close. He bent his arm, with the help of the other, and winced. Reaching out to him, Aeriel said:

"Whereafter shall commence
   such a cruel, sorcerous war
To wrest recompense
   for a land leaguered sore.

With a broadsword bright burning,
   a shadow black as night
From exile returning
   shall champion the fight

For love of one above who, flag unfurled,
   lone must stand,
The pearl of the soul of the world
   in her hand.

When Winterock to water
   falls flooding, foes to drown,

> *Ravenna's own daughter*
> *shall kindle the crown."*

Silence. No sound in the tent but the fizz of lampwicks and the night wind sighing. Her brother Roshka eyed her uncertainly. Syllva stood mute beside her Istern sons. The bewildered sentries glanced at one another. Then she heard Talb the Mage chuckle and Pendarlon begin to purr. But her gaze remained on Irrylath.

"Oh, husband," she breathed, "believe in me."

Coming forward, he knelt before the flame that Erin held. His sword arm seemed nearly recovered now, for with it, he reached toward Aeriel.

"I do," he whispered, "for it is you. Forgive my doubting."

His hand passed through the flame, without harm this time. She experienced a flickering, and the odd feeling of something broad and insubstantial passing through her, but then it was gone, and her vision of Irrylath and the rose silk tent steadied again. Sabr had come to stand beside the prince. She touched his shoulder, mistrust plain upon her face.

"Cousin," she warned. "How can you be sure? We have known for months that Aeriel is lost—

yet now this apparition claims it is not so! Dare you trust the rime that she has given you?"

The prince rose suddenly and turned on her. "Unhand me," he spat, his voice like burning oil. "It was you I let convince me that Aeriel was lost, you I let persuade me to turn from her memory! We have dallied here at desert's edge uncounted hours on your advisement. This is Aeriel. I know her. Do not presume to advise me further, queen of thieves!"

His tone was savage, his expression furious. Aeriel felt an ugly little thread of satisfaction run through her.

"My thought was for *you*," Sabr cried, stumbling back from him as though she had been struck. Her face held a look of desperate betrayal. "Always and ever for *you*!"

Turning, the prince's cousin fled, disappearing into the night. Irrylath watched her go, his expression hard, full of fury still. It was the Lady Syllva who spoke at last, coming forward to touch the prince's arm.

"You are too hard, my son," she reproved him sternly. "Too hard by half. Aeriel is your wife, but Sabr is your cousin still, and a commander in my warhost—your equal in rank. What she says is true: she thinks only of you. *She* has been the one to lead our desert trek, keeping our forces together against desertion and despair, and not two daymonths past, it was she alone that stood between you and your own dagger."

The prince glared at the Lady, but made no reply. Aeriel put one hand to her temple. Her head was spinning. A heavy weariness had begun to steal over her. She had not realized the effort that speaking through the sword required. Perception through it was much more intense than through the pearl, arduous even, sapping her energy. Its strange sensation of heatless burning had hollowed her.

"I must leave you," she said unsteadily. Irrylath and the others turned.

"No!" the prince began, reaching for her again. "Don't go."

She shook her head. "I must. Spanning the distance between us is difficult..., and I have Ravenna's task to fulfill."

"Aeriel," cried Irrylath. "Stay. Stay."

Again she shook her head. She must be gone, at once. The strain was growing dangerous.

"Sheathe the sword, Erin," she whispered. "Be quick."

Irrylath was reaching for her. "Don't—"

"Look for me at the Witch's Mere. Erin!" Aeriel hissed.

"Fare well," the dark girl whispered. "And goodspeed."

In one swift motion, she sheathed the sword, and the sensation of draining ceased. Spent, Aeriel sank to her knees. The Waste stretched flat, grey, and broken around her, misty by pearllight. Her eyelids strayed shut. Hours. It would take hours for the pearl to restore her. She must guard her strength in future. As fatigue dragged fiercely at her, she shook her head. Sleep—she needed sleep. Aeriel lay down upon the cracked and bitter surface of the Waste. The pearl brought her only a faint echo of Irrylath's distant, despairing cry.

"Aeriel!"

It was the last she heard before falling headlong into troubled dreams.

TEN

Winterock

∾

THE NIGHTMARE ENVELOPED HER: THE prince of Avaric falling from the back of his wingèd steed. Dreaming, Aeriel tried to reach out, to reach him, but she could not move. Cold crystal encased her. Frozen, all she could do was watch, shuddering, as Irrylath plunged headfirst through empty air toward roiling nothingness below. *I should have left you your wings,* she thought wildly, despairing. His cry rang in her ears:

"Aeriel!"

Abruptly she woke. Something huge and scaly crouched beside her, picking at her gown with its knifelike claws. With a scream she started up, scrambling back—then stopped herself. The creature before her was not the great monstrous thing she had thought at first, but small and covered with mangy grey down. Illusion cloaked it in a phantom shape, but the pearl now showed her its real form: a long-limbed ratlike thing.

Aeriel struck at it with the flat of her hand. It chittered, blinking at her with bright red eyes before scuttling away. Surely it belonged to the Witch. Aeriel scrambled to her feet and started off again. She felt stronger now—a trace wan yet, but by and large, the pearl had restored her.

Through Erin, she sensed the army, many miles away, breaking camp and proceeding with all speed toward the Mere. Catching a glimpse of Irrylath as he marshaled his mother's Istern forces, Aeriel felt relief flooding her to find him safe still, despite her dream. Sabr rode at the head of her Westron troops, apart from him. Though she sometimes gazed in his direction, the prince refused her so much as a glance. The sight now gave Aeriel little joy. Sabr's stricken face after her cousin's rebuff hours earlier had soured any sense of triumph.

Often, as she journeyed, Aeriel cupped one hand to her brow, hoping somehow to reach into the pearl with her senses and use its sorcery to help her unravel the mystery of Ravenna's cryptic instructions: *Crush the Witch's army. Destroy her darkangels . . . and put the pearl into her hand.* But how? *How?* Surely somewhere within the pearl the answer must lie. But all her efforts proved in vain. The Ancient jewel remained opaque to her, its powers beyond her grasp, and its gifts—of light, nourishment, heightened perception—always unbidden, arriving without summons.

Tempted nearly to despair, Aeriel could only walk on. The parched ground soon grew more broken, cut by dry riverbeds. No plants grew but thirsty, withered scrub. The Waste was more desolate than any place she had ever known. Even the most drought-stricken lands of Westernesse could not compare.

And the Waste was full of the Witch's little nightmare creatures. Cloaked in illusory shape, all appeared at first glance to be monsters. But the pearl soon penetrated their guises, revealing them for the mere vermin that they were. It seemed they could hide anywhere, in the dead scrub, in the cracks. Initially, they dodged her gaze so that Aeriel caught only glimpses. Soon, however, they grew bolder—until before many hours she had a whole raft of them dogging her across the Waste.

Besides the long-legged rat-creatures, whose great protruding front teeth met like those of a horse's skull, she saw odd molelike beasts with dusty, spotted fur, disguised by witchery to appear like ogres. Sometimes little snakes no thicker than her smallest finger hissed at her, miming basilisks. Once or twice a speckled thing resembling a huge moth fluttered after her till she swatted at it. Then it buzzed, a mere bott-fly, and shivered away.

All of them had red orbs, featureless as glass. They were the Witch's eyes, keeping watch on her, Aeriel felt sure. Whenever she paused to rest, they crept closer, stealing up behind her to catch hold of her robe in their little teeth. Though she could neither ignore them nor drive them far away, Ravenna's pearl enabled her to see their true forms beneath the Witch's illusory guises. Plainly intended to terrify, they annoyed her instead. She found their constant presence wearing, but not unnerving.

The stars above wheeled ever so slowly. She knew that she had been walking half the monthlong night. Irrylath and the distant army continued on their convergent path with hers, halting only each dozen hours for food and a few hours' rest. Aeriel herself felt no need now to sleep. In truth, she preferred not, considering what might come upon her unawares.

She reached the cliffs so abruptly that they took her by surprise. One moment, all was silent around her, save for the soughing of a slight, bitter wind and the scrabbling of the phantom creatures. The next, she heard jackals crying—their song floating eerily on the air—and realized what the maze of canyons opening before her must be: the jackal cliffs that never released any wayfarer they swallowed. At the heart of them lay the Witch's Mere.

Aeriel halted, listening to the long, ululating wail of the Witch's dogs. Yips, barks, then silence for a few heartbeats. A single cry rose, clear and falling, to be joined by another voice, then another, and another yet. Abruptly, they stilled, to be followed by silence again. The loathsome creatures clustering about her were growing impatient. Some of them scrabbled ahead, then turned to twitter at her. Unseen jackals sang and wuthered on the wind. Realizing that once she entered, there could be no turning back, Aeriel stepped into the labyrinth.

How long she wandered, she had no way to tell. Only a ribbon of sky showed overhead. Without a horizon, she could not judge how far the stars had turned. The pearl chose her way, distinguishing false trails from true and disregarding illusory walls meant to confuse and conceal the path. An unexpected sense of loss overwhelmed her when she discovered she could no longer sense where the army was. The twisting canyons seemed to bar the pearl's link to the dark girl with the sword.

Then the stone walls fell away on either side, and she was out of the maze. The jackals howled and hooted behind her. The creatures swarming about her ankles chittered and hissed. Before her lay a great flat stretch—tar black, oil smooth, without reflection: the Mere. So this was the place where the Lady Syllva's caravan had found itself trapped so many years ago, this the spot where the boy prince Irrylath had been lured by his nurse to the water's edge and given to the Witch.

Aeriel shuddered, picking her way through the bones that littered the bank. Far in the distance, she saw a white spire rising from the black water: the Witch's palace? It must be—though she had always pictured the whole keep as lying concealed beneath the surface of the lake. She shook her head, wondering how she was to reach it. She dared not touch the poisoned water.

All at once the lake in front of her began to seethe and boil. Aeriel fell back, alarmed. The Witch's creatures milled nervously. Something beneath the surface was rising to the air. A moment later, the huge, pebbled head of a toad broke through. It was pale lavender, almost translucent. Aeriel could not have wrapped her arms about it if she had tried. The creature looked at her with great, bulbous eyes. Its livid tongue, a little ragged flag, threaded along the wrinkled edges of its mouth. The still, black waters obscured all but the creature's head from view.

"So," it said. Its voice boomed like a kettle, like a hunt horn, like a drum. "Another traveler comes to die upon my lady's shore."

Aeriel stared, realizing the identity of the creature: years older now and far more massive, but the same that had once lured the prince's nurse to the Witch's cause and helped her to betray him. Biting back revulsion, Aeriel called out,

"A traveler, mudlick, but not one who has come to die. I would see your mistress and so must cross the lake."

The mudlick cocked one gelid eye.

"How is it you can see me without tasting the Mere?" it boomed. Aeriel touched the pearl upon her brow. The mudlick shifted uneasily, sinking lower in the black water, retracting its pale eyes from the cool, pure light. "You must be the sorceress who has lately caused my lady so very much trouble."

Aeriel nodded. "Will you take me to her?"

The mudlick belched. "My mistress, the White Lady, sees no one."

Aeriel stood disconcerted. She had not expected so quick and final a rebuff. Resolutely, she folded her arms.

"Very well," she replied. "I will not see her, though I have traveled a long road. My message from her mother, the Ancient Ravenna, will go unsaid. Your mistress will thank you for turning me away."

She spun on her heel and started back toward the jackal cliffs. The scrabbling creatures scattered before her. She had gotten three steps when the mudlick called, "Wait."

Aeriel turned but did not approach. She saw the monstrous thing's forelegs in the water now. They seemed oddly small for its great bulk. It nibbled one of its fingers.

"You are a sorceress," it mused. "Why do you not use your sorcery to cross?"

Because I have no sorcery! Aeriel wanted to cry, but she held her tongue.

"Take me across, or not, exactly as you please," she said at last. She had no more patience left.

The mudlick sighed and lapped at the black,

poisonous waters. "My mistress would not thank me for bringing her bane."

"As you please," Aeriel snapped, turning on her heel once more. "I leave you to your lady's wrath when she discovers you repelled her mother's messenger." She counted the paces. One. Two.

"Oh, very well!" the creature cried after her. "Have it your own way. I will take you across to my mistress's keep—just in case what you say might be true—though whether she will let you in, I cannot say. Wade out," it told her, rising higher under the Mere's shadowy surface.

Aeriel recoiled. "I won't touch the water."

The mudlick laughed, a deep gonging sound like hot, hammered metal. It heaved itself from the black, unnaturally calm waters, dragging itself up onto the bank. The dark moisture seemed less to run off its skin than to boil away in a thin vapor. Swallowing her revulsion, Aeriel approached and climbed to crouch just behind the great toad's head, uncertain how much of its body would sink back beneath the Mere. Its pebbled skin, covered with great slippery warts, was cold and had an oily feel.

"It's been a dracg's age since I last ate," the

mudlick remarked, surveying the little creatures before it on the bank.

With a motion so quick Aeriel could scarcely follow, its vast jaws gaped, and its long tongue swept out, catching up a dozen of the frantically scattering vermin—along with a great quantity of the bank. The mudlick's jaws snapped shut. It laughed and swallowed, bloated sides heaving. Sickened, Aeriel held on desperately as her porter hauled itself around and slid back into the Mere.

"Stupid things," it croaked.

The black waters curled around its snout and trailed along its sides. Aeriel snatched one foot higher to avoid the Mere's touch. The mudlick bobbed, and Aeriel swallowed hard. She caught glimpses of other creatures in the lake around them, though none showed their heads above the glass-smooth surface. Once, they passed over something so long and huge she gasped.

"That is only a mereguint," the toad told her, "one of my lady's water dragons. She has two: great enough to swallow ships. If you should fall in, little messenger, they will make short work of you."

A vision filled Aeriel's mind of the treacherous mudlick rearing back to dump her into the teem-

ing Mere for sheer sport. She clutched tighter to
the great toad's back.

"See me safe to the palace," she warned, "or
you will answer to your mistress for it. I bear
Ravenna's gift for her, more precious than my
life."

The mudlick only laughed. Aeriel realized it
could feel her shaking—for even without the
dragons, she was terrified, and not just of the enchanted water, but of any water. She could not
swim, and so clung to the mudlick with all her
might. It swam steadily on. The great castle hove
nearer, rising up from the Mere. These spires
could be only the top, she thought in awe, only
the tiniest tip of an enormous keep. The rest lay
below the lake. Again the mudlick's booming
chuckle.

"You thought it would all be underwater, didn't
you? Used to be, not many years past. But it's
grown so, she can't keep it all beneath the surface
now."

One eye swiveled to look at her. Aeriel managed to glare back. As the mudlick brought her
to the edge of the crystal keep, Aeriel scrambled
off in relief onto a narrow terrace a few inches
above the waterline. To her astonishment, she

found that the ledge was cold, far colder than the mudlick's skin. Glass smooth, it was so chill the soles of her feet adhered to it. Uneasily, she shifted from foot to foot. What stone, what jewel had been used to make this tower? The pearl upon her brow brightened, suffusing her with warmth.

"Well, little sorceress," boomed the mudlick, "I have brought you here. Now enter if you can."

With a final deep laugh, it sank from sight below the surface of the Mere. Nightshade was very late. From the tilt of the stars, she saw that it must be nearly Solstarrise. She shifted her feet once more to keep the soles from binding to the stone. If not for the pearl, she realized, the cold would have been unbearable. Gazing up at the blank, unbroken white walls of the palace, she began to walk along the landing, searching for a door.

SHE WALKED UNTIL SHE FELT DIZZY, HER neck stiff, but she could find no window, no portal, no chink or opening. At last she stopped, baffled and exhausted. Desperation ate at her. Somehow she must get in. She had not come all this way to be turned back now. Aeriel felt an odd stirring in the back of her mind, a low, almost unintelligible murmuring.

Place your hand against the stone, it seemed to

whisper—so softly that in the next instant, she was not even sure it had spoken at all. Nevertheless, she placed one palm against the frigid surface, gingerly, lest it stick. Nothing happened. Frustration welled in her. She pressed harder, heedless now, throwing her whole weight against the keep. *Open,* she cried silently, angrily. *Let me in!*

The stone surface beneath her hand abruptly vanished. Aeriel stumbled forward. Catching her balance, she spun around to behold the outer wall now parted in a broad archway. Pearllight gleamed on the clear, white crystal of the palace interior. Aeriel touched the jewel upon her brow again, astonished. Even as she watched, the wall seamed soundlessly together once more, forestalling retreat.

She stood in a deserted hallway. Starlight filtered in through the crystalline walls. Despite the pearl's warmth, she was shivering hard. The fierce cold of the Witch's keep numbed her. Her breath came in gasps, swirling up in puffs like scentless smoke. Something told her she would be well enough as long as she kept moving. Though the pearl's power was great, it was subtle. She must not pause, must not rest. Aeriel started down the long, empty hall.

The walls around her were uneven but smooth,

in some places nearly transparent. Sometimes she sensed she was passing along the outer wall of the keep and what lay beyond was open sky. It must be nearing Solstarrise by now, she knew. Her breath, when she leaned closer, seeking to peer beyond the ripples, fogged the crystal stone. Once she brushed against it in passing, and the dry cold adhered to her like something tacky and alive. She had to snatch her arm away.

Her path led mostly downward at first, so that after a time she was certain she had passed below the waterline. The stone of the wall was clearer here. Beyond, the dark waters of the Mere moved sluggishly. A flock of hatchet-shaped swimming things darted past, their huge mouths gaping. Something long and grey slid after them, doubling back on itself. It snapped bladelike teeth at her. Aeriel jumped. Farther out, something much vaster circled, very black: one of the Witch's mereguints, a water dragon. Aeriel hastened on.

Journeying deeper, she passed through mazes of corridors with faceted walls, each throwing her image back at her until she halted, baffled, scarcely able to tell where her own form ended and her reflection began. Always the pearl guided her onward and through. Once, at a juncture of two hallways, she sensed that if she had taken the other

fork, it would have led inevitably down to where
the captured duaroughs labored, deep in the palace
bowels, beneath even the mud bottom of the Mere.

Many rooms flanked the corridor—all empty
now. Unbidden, the pearl's sight revealed to her
more than she wanted to know about the past of
those deserted chambers. Here the Witch's black
birds had flocked. There she had built her darkangels' wings, and in another, gilded their hearts
with lead. The pearl observed the palace's memories with relentless dispassion. Shuddering, the
pale girl covered her face with her hands. How
could any mortal being have become so corrupt?
Could anyone capable of such evil ever be redeemed? What might the pearl of the soul of the
world become in the hands of such a one?

And yet, she remembered the Ancient's words,
she is my daughter still.

Aeriel came to a room which halted her. Without looking, she sensed what lay beyond the door:
a siege as white as salt, such as a queen might
sit enthroned upon. The pearl imparted to her a
glimpse from the chamber's past: the young Irrylath, not yet a darkangel, brought to his knees
before that siege. The silver chain encircling his
wrist was grasped in the hand of the tall, seated
woman before him. She leaned forward, her face

bowed from view. Her other hand was a fist in the young man's hair. Cruelly, she forced his head back, bending to whisper in his ear:

"Yes, love. You *will*."

Aeriel cried out. The sound shivered down the length of the empty hall, rebounding and magnifying into a louder and louder shriek, until it seemed that not one voice but many screamed. Aeriel ducked, covering her ears. She had no idea of the context of that scene—what had happened before it or followed after—and little cared. Her attention remained fixed on the horror of a single point in time: of the young Irrylath defying his mistress, and the White Witch slowly, inexorably—relishing every moment of it—breaking him to her will.

Aeriel gasped for breath and bit off her cries.

"No," she told herself sternly. "No!"

That glimpse which the pearl had brought her came from the past. It was not happening now. Half breathless, she uncovered her ears and heard the many blade-thin echoes dying.

" '*Love*,' " she whispered, remembering the lorelei's words to Irrylath. Shaking, Aeriel gazed around her at the cold, white walls. "Nothing in this frozen place has anything to do with love!"

Grimly, she padded forward. The path wound

on and on, sometimes downward, sometimes level. Eventually, she began to travel upward again. It must be long past Solstarrise, she realized, no longer night outside. No inkling of dawn had reached her before, but the light was much brighter since she had once more risen above the dark waterline. She had the sense of being far higher now than when she had entered the palace.

"How long have I been wandering here?" she wondered.

A broad, straight corridor stretched before her. She halted, trembling, dimly aware suddenly of what lay ahead of her and not wanting to go on. She stood a long time, reaching out through the senses of the pearl, trying desperately to find another path—to no avail. Here lay the only path. Aeriel drew a ragged breath.

Quickly, she forced herself ahead down the long corridor. Human figures stood embedded in the walls on either side of her. None of them moved. Still as stone every one, caught fast in the indescribably cold crystal. Their eyes were all closed, all their limbs and faces frozen in attitudes of horror, struggle, revulsion, and despair. And yet, even so, the pearl told her, they were alive. Were they even physical bodies at all, or were they souls—captured by the Witch and her darkangels but not yet devoured? Unnerved, Aeriel ran on.

The corridor ended in an open archway. A blaze of Solstarlight lay beyond. She saw a window, unshuttered, unglazed. The wind blowing in off the Waste was stiff, made thin by altitude. Panting, her breath swirling in clouds, Aeriel halted in the wash of sunlight streaming in. Its warmth felt delicious. She savored it. The lateness of the hour outside dismayed her: Solstar hung low. She had entered the Witch's keep before dawn.

"There you are," said a cold, clear voice. It rang like crystal, like a bell. Like a darkangel's voice: rich, compelling, clear. "At last. Well. Through my palace of Winterock, it is not always easy to find one's way."

Winterock. Aeriel could not tell if the word named the palace itself or the frigid stone from which it was formed. The speaker laughed, deeply, languidly.

"But I never doubted you would find me, little sorceress."

ELEVEN

Heart of Dust

THE CHILL THAT POURED THROUGH AERIEL as she listened to that voice vanquished the warmth of Solstar. Turning, she saw the White Witch standing not far from the casement: her vantage from which to watch the coming battle, Aeriel guessed. Across the small chamber, Oriencor appraised her coolly. She was very tall, almost as tall as Ravenna, but whereas the Ancient had been a dark lady, all dusk and black and indigo, her daughter the White Witch was fair.

Her skin was as pale as Irrylath's had been when Aeriel had known him as a darkangel: bone white without any rose to the cheeks or lips, no blush of blood. Her frigid breath did not cloud the air. Her features were sharp and angular, coldly beautiful, like a merciless statue. Only her eyes had any color, pale green. A sorceress's eyes. The Witch's hair was long and white, straighter than Ravenna's. Colorless filament. Darkangel hair.

Her lips were thin, bowed, curling upward at the corners in malevolent amusement. She was wearing a long white gown that fell close about her figure, clinging to it. It was sewn with little bits of things: dogs' teeth, cut diamonds, and freshwater pearls—twisted and baroque in shape, not round. Cats' claws and buttons of bone. Aeriel could not see the lorelei's feet. Her gown dragged the floor. Her white nails were very long and keen. Before her Aeriel felt stupid, clumsy, weak —as though the other could, with but a glance, read her to the heart.

Shivering, she answered, "I am not a sorceress."

The White Witch smiled. Her teeth were pointed, sharp as little spades.

"Perhaps not," she said, drawing nearer. The cold breathed from her as from a high mountainside in shadow. "But you have been a great difficulty to me. And you have lately visited my mother in NuRavenna. Tell me, is she well?"

"She's dead," said Aeriel, shaking, refusing to retreat.

She remembered vividly—the last breath of the

Ancientlady fading and the dark man bending his grief-stricken face to her hair. Ravenna's fair daughter laughed, wholly self-possessed, a bell-like, mocking sound.

"You are so earnest," she sighed. "I should not play with you. I know that she is dead. I saw the beacon of her funeral fire."

Aeriel stared at her. The coldness with which the other spoke astonished her. One swansdown eyebrow lifted.

"Do I shock you, little Aeriel, rejoicing in my own mother's death?"

Aeriel saw that one of the trinkets stitched to her gown was the mummified foot of some very small white creature: a lizard, a mole? Oriencor clenched one dagger-nailed hand. Her fingers were webbed, Aeriel realized suddenly. Gills slitted behind her ears.

"Fool. She could have made herself immortal, like me—if she had dared. Now her own mortality has claimed her at last, and the world is mine."

She spoke with such unflinching authority that Aeriel's hand went to the jewel at her brow, seeking reassurance—then froze there as the lorelei fastened her glass-green gaze upon the pearl.

"My mother gave you a gift, I see."

Terror swept through Aeriel as she realized that

very soon she must give up the pearl. She had worn Ravenna's jewel so long she had almost forgotten existence without it. And yet, she told herself sternly, the pearl did not belong to her. It was meant for the world's heir. Still, the thought of parting with it was agony.

"A boon," she managed at last.

"A message capsule, by the look," the Witch remarked, as though not greatly interested. "After all these years, what could my mother possibly have to say to me?"

Aeriel shook her head. How to explain? Where to begin? She found her tongue growing thick and awkward in her mouth. Touching the pearl still, she could only manage, "Ravenna bade me bring it to you."

Oriencor shrugged. "How charming. But you keep it awhile, little sorceress, lest the cold kill you too soon. Time enough for me to savor my mother's dying breath after the battle." She smiled her wolfish smile. "After I've slaughtered all your people and devoured their souls."

Aeriel's knees grew weak. The other's voice was at once lovely and terrible, seductive to listen to. Aeriel felt the moment—her chance to confront and persuade the Witch—slipping away. She drew breath to make some desperate last appeal—

but a soft, inner voice intervened. *Let it go,* the voice murmured, already fading. *Now is not the time. Not yet, but soon.*

"Come," the lorelei said. "Watch the battle with me. It is about to be joined."

She beckoned Aeriel to a window. The sill there dripped with water in the sunlight's blaze.

"See them below us," Oriencor murmured. "Your forces and mine. All assembled. All arrayed. The victory will be mine, of course. It will be a pleasure to watch. I know so few pleasures these days. Watch with me."

Aeriel saw armies on the strand below. The small chamber in which she and Oriencor stood was indeed at a great height. The Witch's brood were massed upon the shore: jackals and weasel-hounds and black birds; great, hunched creatures of vaguely human shape; and thin, wraithlike figures—rank upon rank of them, so many she could not count. The black waters of the Mere behind them teemed with more. Aeriel spotted the mudlick, bobbing near shore, and deeper out, circling the palace, the two enormous wakes of the Witch's water dragons.

Syllva's forces faced the Mere, fanned out in a crescent. Aeriel's heart lifted at the sight of them —only to tighten suddenly as, for the first time,

she perceived how pitifully small their numbers
were in comparison to the Witch's vast horde.
Above the allied warhost, a long yellow banner
turned and fluttered on the breeze. The Lady
stood foremost, surrounded by her bowwomen.
Irrylath rode nearby, astride the wingèd Avarclon. Marelon, the Lithe Serpent of the Sea-of-
Dust, undulated huge and vermilion, her vast coils
lost among the throng. Erin stood farther back,
the lyon Pendarlon pacing beside her. Aeriel saw
the dark girl touch his mane. Beside her at the
windowsill, Oriencor stirred.

"You have all been such a trial to me these last
few dozen daymonths," she sighed, "resisting my
conquest, refusing to acquiesce. I suppose I must
be grateful, though: you assuaged my boredom."

Aeriel turned to see her gazing down hungrily
at the prince of Avaric very far below. The White
Witch smiled.

"Irrylath was the best. He was never boring.
All of six years old when I procured him—too
old, really, to ever come completely to heel. But
that is why I loved him so. So independent! So
surprising. It took me years to tame him."

A hot flame of anger rose in Aeriel. For a moment, it rivaled the warmth of the pearl. She remembered the brief glimpse the pearl had shown

her: Oriencor, one fist in the young Irrylath's hair, commanding him ever so quietly, *Yes, love. You will.* Recklessly, Aeriel drew breath again to speak, but the other's merciless eyes turned and fixed her like a hawk's.

"I will never forgive you for taking him from me," the White Witch breathed, "even for a little time. And I will have him back again. Before I drink his soul away, he will be mine."

Aeriel's skin flushed. "He will never belong to you again," she gasped. "He's *mine*. He loathes you."

Oriencor laughed. "He loves me. And I him."

"You don't," spat Aeriel. "You only want to rule him!" Memory of the lorelei's black birds tormenting her prisoners came back to Aeriel. She shuddered, sickened, and shoved the thought away. "You and your kind don't love anything. I don't think you can."

The Witch's smile soured. Her voice grew petulant, annoyed. "I loved the Ancients once," she murmured, "when I was young. I was capable of love then. But they left me."

Leaning back against the sill, studying Aeriel, Oriencor toyed with the low collar of her gown, stroking her own breastbone. Slowly, Aeriel realized what it was she fingered: a little seam running down, sewn up with silver, just like the one on Irrylath's breast when he had been a darkangel. Oriencor's bloodless lips pursed fretfully.

"It's true," she mused. "I can't love. I don't have a heart of flesh anymore. I took it out, after the Ancients deserted me, and replaced it with one of winterock."

She glanced over one shoulder. Aeriel followed her gaze. A crystal box rested in a niche across the room.

"I put the original away for safekeeping."

Warily, Aeriel eyed the box. Something dark lay inside, dimly visible through the colorless stone. Oriencor shrugged.

"You may look at it, if you wish."

The pearl burned bright upon her brow. Aeriel felt an irresistible attraction drawing her to the box. Slowly, she crossed the room and touched the lid. The crystal was bone chill: cold as the keep.

"Don't think you can harm it," the lorelei warned, still at the windowsill. "I'd never let you near it, if you could do it any harm."

Aeriel felt a stirring within the pearl, like something just beginning to wake—but it subsided at once. She lifted the box's lid and halted, frowning.

Nothing lay within the box but a layer of fine, dark grit. Immediately, the pearl brightened.

"There's nothing in here," she said. "Nothing but dust."

Scowling, Ravenna's daughter bit her lip with one pointed tooth. "Won't you lie to flatter me, little sorceress?" she inquired. "Aren't you afraid of me yet?"

Aeriel turned to face her. "I'm very much afraid of you," she answered. No use to pretend otherwise. The Ancient's daughter could read her with such ease. Still biting her lip, the White Witch smiled.

"So was Irrylath. And he said the same."

Despite the other's eyes upon her, Aeriel felt her own gaze, very gently, being directed once more to the fine sooty stuff in the bottom of the box, like ashes of the dead. Within the pearl, something shifted again. She reached to touch the ash. It was cool and clung together like barely damp meal. Ravenna's pearl glowed. A strange, soft murmuring came into the back of Aeriel's mind. She tried to listen, but Oriencor's muttered words drowned it out.

"All the others told me what a fine heart it was, how beautifully preserved. They thought to please me. Irrylath told me it was only wormwood. It's why he was my favorite. Of all the boys I ever made into darkangels, only Irrylath never lied."

The Witch's knifelike nails drummed the crystal of the windowsill, chipping and scoring it. They sounded like death beetles clicking in the walls. *Taste it*, the pearl was telling her, *that I may know my daughter's heart*. Almost without a thought, Aeriel touched a few grains of the Witch's dust to her tongue, and a sharp sensation went through her like a pinprick. It was the bitterest thing she had ever known. It tasted like despair. The pearl dimmed then, and its voice subsided. Aeriel forgot about it instantly as a sleeper, waking, forgets a dream. Across the room from her, Oriencor sighed.

"My heart fell away into dust long ago. I hadn't realized it would do that when I cut it out. The crystal was supposed to preserve it. Well, I was very young at sorcery then. But no matter. A heart would be too great a burden to bear with me across the Void."

Aeriel frowned, having lost the other's train of thought. Across the Void? But Oriencor only laughed and turned back to the window.

"Ah," she said softly. "So it starts."

Aeriel caught in her breath. Hastily she replaced the Witch's box in its niche and went to join Oriencor at the casement.

"Your lady's army comes forward," the lorelei murmured.

Gazing down, Aeriel saw the great crescent advancing now, comprising allies of every hue: blue Berneans, pale green Zambulans, Pirseans with coppery skin, pale Terraineans and gold-complected refugees from Avaric, the rose-skinned people of Rani and the teal-colored folk of Elver, dark Mariners, Isterners with plum-colored skin, and the cinnamon-colored wanderers of the desert lands. All at once, Aeriel understood what their yellow banner was. Above them all, her wedding sari floated, blazing in the light of Solstar.

Beside her at the window, Oriencor lifted her gaze. Wingèd figures—half a dozen of them— poised in the air about the keep. Smiling, she commanded them: "Begin."

TWELVE

Seventh Son

෨

WITH A START, AERIEL TOOK NOTE FOR the first time of those to whom the Witch had spoken. High above the palace hovered six dark-angels: manlike but deathly pallid of skin. Their eyes had no color; their flesh was all fallen in. They were bloodless, heartless, soulless things. The dozen black wings upon the back of each icarus thrashed in a furious, silent storm. At Oriencor's signal, precisely as hawks, they turned and fell through the air toward the approaching army below.

Aeriel saw the distant Irrylath unsheathe his Edge Adamantine. Behind him, Syllva's arm swept up, then dropped. The yellow banner dipped, and with a shout, the Istern and Westron troops surged to meet the Witch's host upon the shore. Aeriel saw the wingèd lons taking to the air, unbridled Avarclon among them. With Irrylath astride him, the starhorse sprang aloft, his silver wings flashing as the darkangels swept lower. Then the two armies came together, and all was a wash of confusion.

How long she stood watching, Aeriel had no notion. Solstar seemed to stand still in the sky. The pearl brought her snatches and glimpses of battle, far more vivid and detailed than if she had watched with eyes alone: two of the Witch's creatures locked in combat with a man of Elver, a girl of Zambul and her companion fighting a cluster of eyeless trolls with daggers. She saw the Lady Syllva surrounded by her bowwomen, harassed by a relentless swarm of black birds. Despite the rhuks, the Istern women sent volley after volley of arrows over their own forces' heads into the midst of the enemy beyond. Halfway across the field, the Ma'a-mbai and other wanderers of the dunes wielded their walking sticks, engaged in furious battle with the Witch's spotted jackals.

The field spread out below Aeriel like a great patternless sea of animate beads, surging and breaking against itself in waves. Yet while Syllva's fighters could act only individually, following as best they could the shouted orders of their commanders and the blare of warhorns, the Witch's forces were much more tightly controlled, despite Aeriel's being able to discern among them no apparent communication. She wondered how they knew where to go, what to do.

Soon the pale girl found herself trembling as she began to observe a pattern in the shifting tapestry below. Over and over, she saw contingents of Syllva's forces preparing to close in on pockets of the foe—yet almost inevitably, the enemy pulled back and escaped, though they could not possibly have seen the closing trap from their position on the ground. Abruptly, Aeriel became aware of Oriencor whispering.

"Right turn, *forward*, all of you. Hurry! Hack your way through or you'll be cut off. Captain of rhuks, take wing. Harry the bowwomen. Wheel, hard to the right, left flank. Trolls, forward, *now....*"

The Witch's eyes were riveted, her concentration fierce. She was not watching single fighters as, in the beginning, Aeriel had done. Of that Aeriel grew more and more sure. The White Witch was watching the pattern—no, she was weaving the pattern! The pale girl listened in growing horror. Could Oriencor really be controlling every warrior in her huge warhost? Were they all her catspaws—was her power so great? Staring down at the battlefield, Aeriel felt cold panic nearly overwhelm her.

Gradually, unwillingly, Syllva's troops were losing ground. Over their heads wheeled Irrylath, shouting orders, sounding his warhorn, directing reinforcements wherever need was greatest. His bridleless mount, the Avarclon, dashed foes to the ground and skewered them with his horn. The little ones, he caught in his teeth. Horse and rider seemed tireless, plunging and striking again and again till the Witch's creatures fled before them. Yet step by hard-fought step, the lorelei's vast hoard was forcing the smaller army back, crushing the wings of the crescent, crowding the allies so that they had no room to turn or swing their weapons.

Irrylath called to his steed to take him higher, surveying the fray. Below him, Sabr and her bandits battled, trying to break clear of the surrounding vise. Dirks and half-swords flashing, they made short, ferocious charges to drive the enemy back. A swarm of trolls closed in suddenly behind Sabr, severing her from the main body of her cavalry. Her bodyguard wheeled and hacked, hard-pressed.

Without hesitation, the prince swooped to her

rescue, cutting down half a dozen of her attackers and scattering the rest. Cheering, the riders of Avaric sprang to fill the gap. Aeriel's heart clenched. She did not know whether to rejoice or weep. Surely she had no love for the bandit queen—yet because of her, the allied forces now had a chance to win free. Fighting forward again, Sabr gazed up at Irrylath. For barely a moment, he returned her gaze before, without a word, he wheeled away.

Aeriel spotted the prince's half brothers now, engaging the Witch's darkangels: Nar, the eldest, astride the black wolf Bernalon, fought the icarus of Bern while Arat upon the cockatrice of Elver battled the darkangel of that land. Lern, Syril, and Poratun upon their wingèd mounts dived and circled above, each pursuing his airborne foe.

Below them, her own brother Roshka sat fighting side to side with Hadin, the youngest Istern prince. Two fair-haired cousins as like as like, they looked mirror images of one another: very fierce and serious and utterly without fear. Bestriding the stag of Pirs, the Lady's son swung determinedly at the wingèd witchson with his hook-bladed falchion. Beside him, upon the black steed Nightwalker, Roshka guarded his back.

Dismayed, Aeriel feared them both dangerously vulnerable—until she discerned that wingless mounts actually gave them the advantage. While his brothers veered and tangled in the air above, scarcely able to land a blow, earthbound Hadin forced his icarus again and again to swoop close to the ground, within reach of his weapon and Roshka's. Without warning, an arrow shaft made of gold buried itself in the darkangel's side. Aeriel caught a glimpse of the Lady Syllva lowering her bow.

One of Talb the Mage's arrows tipped with Ancients' silver, she realized, though the arrowhead was already hidden deep in the unbleeding flesh of the darkangel. The bloodless creature screamed and writhed overhead. Roshka hooked it with his pike and hauled it closer. Hadin thrust his falchion to the hilt in the icarus's chest, silencing its scream. As it crumpled out of the air, a great shout went up from the forces of East and West: their first great victory of the day. Elation filled Aeriel. Beside her, Oriencor bared her teeth in a snarl.

"Enough!" she growled. "Enough of this dalliance. Time to make war in earnest now."

The Witch's ivory talons bit deep into Aeriel's shoulder. A chill like none she had ever known swept through her. The pearl dimmed, fighting the Witch's cold. Aeriel gasped and struggled as Oriencor dragged her from the window.

"Tell me, little sorceress," she whispered savagely, halting before the near wall of the tower chamber. "How many sons have I?"

"None," Aeriel flung back. "You are barren."

The Witch's grasp tightened. Her lips turned down. "True," she said. "But there are those who, could they speak, would call themselves my sons. How many icari have I?"

"Six," Aeriel gasped. "Counting the one that Hadin killed." The cold devoured her. Her shoulder was already numb. "You had seven," she managed defiantly, "but Irrylath is lost to you."

Oriencor muttered, "We shall see. But did I hear you say I have but six darkangels? You are mistaken. I have seven."

"No!" Aeriel cried. "Irrylath is *mine....*"

The White Witch shook her head, smiling now. "I do not refer to Irrylath. You have seen my other six upon the field—each fighting one of your husband's brothers. But you have not yet seen my newest icarus, the one I made *after* Irrylath, just this twelvemonth past."

Aeriel stared at her. What was she saying—a new darkangel? A seventh son?

"You have not had time—" she stammered.
The chill made her teeth rattle, her jaw ache. She
writhed in the other's grasp. Even Ravenna's
pearl, she realized, could not long protect her
against such killing cold. The White Witch gave
her a little shake.

"How naive you are."

Desperately, Aeriel searched her memory. She
knew the lorelei stole infants, babes-in-arms whom
she raised to young manhood before drinking their
blood and gilding their hearts with lead, planting
a dozen night-black pinions on their backs and
sending them out to prey upon the world. The
pale girl protested:

"It takes years to make a darkangel!"

Oriencor sighed. "To do a proper job, perhaps.
But I have grown impatient of late. Irrylath, you
recall, I acquired as a child of six. I kept him
mortal only ten years before I winged him."

Aeriel's eyes widened. She had saved Irrylath
before Oriencor could make him into a full-
fledged icarus—but what was to have prevented
Oriencor from stealing another child and render-
ing him at once into one of her unspeakable
"sons"? Reading the memories of Winterock, the
pearl brought images, sure and certain, into
Aeriel's mind: the lorelei building a new set of

child-sized wings, gilding a small, fresh heart with lead. Grimly, the White Witch nodded.

"Irrylath's replacement," she said. "My new 'son' has never flown, but it is high time now. Your husband's warhost is having far too easy a time."

Slow dread filled Aeriel. She stared at the wall in front of her. The palm of Oriencor's hand just hovered above its translucent surface. A hair-thin crack ran down the wall—so fine Aeriel would never have seen it without the aid of the pearl. She heard rustling, glimpsed movement through the stone. As Oriencor laid her hand at last upon the crack, it parted smoothly, forming a doorway so low and narrow only a child could easily pass through. The White Witch smiled.

"Time for Irrylath to meet *his* darkangel."

A creature shaped like a human child stood in a cavity beyond the door: a parody of human form, its skin stretched dead white over sunken flesh. A dozen black wings draped its shoulders. Still caught in the Witch's grasp, Aeriel shrank away. Nothing about this thing was beautiful— unlike Irrylath when she had first known him as an unfinished icarus. In contrast, this creature seemed an automaton. It spoke no word, moved stiffly as though made of wax: an utter darkangel. The Witch had already drunk away its soul.

"Golam," Aeriel whispered, shaking uncontrollably with the cold. "Animate doll!"

"Yes."

Turning its colorless eyes toward her, the white-faced creature hissed. Delighted, Oriencor laughed.

"So, chick. Ready to fly? One of your fellows is dead," she told it. "It only makes the rest of you dearer to me. To the casement. Haste! Your task's at hand."

Shifting as though uneasy, the creature continued to eye Aeriel. It seemed reluctant to approach. As Oriencor's daggerlike nails dug into Aeriel's flesh, her knees went weak, her whole side now numb. She winced, biting back a cry.

"Oh, don't mind her, you stupid thing," the White Witch snapped. "She can't really hurt you with those eyes."

The little darkangel swept past then, gargling at Aeriel still. It bounded to the window and sprang onto the wet, watery sill, where it crouched, wings flexing like a young bird's, fanning the air. Oriencor shoved Aeriel abruptly away from her, and the pale girl staggered, falling

to her knees. The little icarus whistled and yam-
mered. Striding to the window ledge, the White
Witch transfixed it with her gaze.

"Fly now," she commanded, "and bring me
Irrylath."

Languidly, carelessly, the White Witch kissed
her hissing, snarling creature and pushed it off the
ledge. The darkangel's wings began their storm-
like, circular motion as it sped away across the air,
flying as though it had known flight all its life.
Crumpled against the wall, Aeriel struggled vainly
to rise. Upon her brow the pearl flickered, nearly
spent. *Get up,* something within murmured urgently. *Rise now, or you never will!* With great
effort, Aeriel dragged herself to her feet.

Panting, she leaned unsteadily against the wall.
Through the casement, she saw Oriencor's seventh
darkangel swooping across the sky toward where
Irrylath hovered, calling something down to the
Lady Syllva among the bowwomen of Isternes.
One of them looked up and caught her comman-
der's arm, pointing. Syllva turned, then Irrylath.
Sweat-stained and grave, the prince looked weary
but not frightened. He had not yet realized what
this icarus was.

Pointing with his Blade, he spoke a word to the

Avarclon. But as the bridleless starhorse wheeled, climbing the air, his rider suddenly recoiled. Aeriel beheld bewilderment, and then open dismay, break over his face. The wingèd Horse never checked his ascent as Irrylath cast wildly about him, counting darkangels. The little icarus stooped. Astonished, the prince spun in the saddle to face the Witch's new "son."

It dipped low first, harrying Avarclon. With a scream of rage, the starhorse struck at the child-shaped thing, but it dodged away. Irrylath lunged in the saddle, but the icarus pivoted, swooping upward from below to bait the prince's mount. Again Avarclon plunged and once more struck only empty air. The starhorse shook his head, pawing the sky, trumpeting his fury. Face grim, Irrylath swung recklessly, repeatedly, lightning swift, but each time, the little icarus deftly evaded him, its dozen dark wings fanning like a storm. It seemed to have no wish to engage with him, only to taunt—hovering just out of range.

Weak with cold, Aeriel shuddered. Before her at the window, Oriencor stood laughing. Abruptly, the pale girl noticed that without Irrylath to command them from the air, the allied forces below had begun to waver. The Witch's smile twitched. Aeriel stared as those beautiful white lips began to move as if in speech, but no sound emerged. Instead, it was the darkangel that spoke. The heightened perception of the pearl conveyed the sound clearly to Aeriel even at this distance: the little icarus mouthing the words of its mistress in a high, locustlike singsong.

"Come back to me," the wingèd witch-child said. "Though I speak with another's voice, know that it is I, Oriencor."

Irrylath started, staring at the little darkangel. A strangled cry escaped his lips.

"You loved me once," Oriencor's catspaw droned. "Do you not love me still, who mothered you after your own dam deserted you? I who gave you wings? I will give you wings again—such wings!—if only you will return to me."

Stumbling, Aeriel groped her way to the window. Oblivious, silently whispering, Oriencor never turned.

"Behold the one I have made to take your place among my darkangels," she breathed, and the little icarus repeated her words. "For you have proved yourself worthy of a far grander rank. Be my consort! Return and sit beside me upon the siege as white as salt. Rule the world with me."

"No," Aeriel whispered, weak still, her breath coming short. "Husband, no!"

Irrylath sat gazing at the soulless thing before him as one mesmerized. The vampyre child whirred nearer, still just out of reach. Avarclon could only tread air, snorting with fury, unable to strike. The White Witch's fingernails grated on the slick, dripping sill.

"Come back," she crooned. The icarus echoed her. "You love me still. Admit it. You love me still."

Irrylath shuddered, breathing hard. Aeriel clung desperately to the cold, wet window ledge.

"Don't listen!" she gasped.

But his eyes were fastened on the darkangel. It floated before him, filling his gaze. Though the pearl enhanced Aeriel's senses enough to see and hear what passed between Irrylath and the darkangel, she knew her own weak protests could never hope to reach him. Clearly the White Witch's words in the darkangel's mouth were the only ones he heard.

"You are mine and you know it, and always have been. You came all this way not to destroy me but to bring me souls! Look at your followers scattered below you. How small they are! How high above them you ride. They cannot stop you from rejoining me now. Come, my love. Give me your hand. My seventh son will pluck you away to me."

Like a man in a dream, Irrylath lowered the Edge Adamantine. The little darkangel fluttered nearer, fixing him with its colorless eyes. If the prince had reached out, he could almost have touched it. The breath of its wings stirred his long, black hair. Oriencor sighed, laughing. She had him.

"No!" Aeriel screamed. "Irrylath—"

She might as well have tried to outshout the wind. Her words were lost in the clamor of battle. Horrified, she remembered her nightmare: Irrylath falling headlong toward oblivion. She could not save him. *I should never have stolen your heart,* she thought wildly, bitterly. *I should have let you die in Avaric—it was what you wanted—rather than bring you here for the Witch to claim!* Tears burned on her cheeks, hardening as they cooled. She brushed at them distractedly, and they fell like little beads of colorless stone.

At the casement, Oriencor murmured silkily, "Come back to me, my own sweet son. Come, love. Son. Come."

Battle below had come almost to a standstill,

all eyes fixed on Irrylath above. The prince's darkangel hovered within reach now, holding out its hand. Slowly, Irrylath raised his own—hesitated—then in one swift lunge, he caught the inhuman thing before him by the wrist. With a cry of triumph or of agony, he dragged the Witch's golam down against the frantic beating of its wings and plunged the Blade Adamantine into its breast.

THIRTEEN

Dragons

PIERCED TO ITS LEADEN HEART, THE little darkangel fell, wings stiff, feathers fluttering like rags. Aeriel felt giddy, light. Irrylath had not returned to Oriencor! Leaning against the casement for support, Aeriel felt that she might die of happiness as, without a ripple, the lifeless body of the Witch's seventh son disappeared into the still, black waters of the Mere. Avarclon gave a great neigh of victory, and a shout went up from the army of the allies below. Irrylath wheeled to face Oriencor.

"I will *not* come back to you, Witch," he shouted. "I serve the Aeriel now."

"Have a care, my one-time love," she answered savagely, seizing her prisoner and dragging her into the prince's view. "Your Aeriel is in my hands."

The pale girl saw him start.

"Aeriel!" he cried. Beneath him, Avarclon wheeled sharp in the air, his great wings beating. Oriencor laughed.

"Fool," she spat. "If you had come back, I'd have given her to you. Now I will keep her for myself. She will die very slowly at the end of this war. As will you."

Rage swept over Irrylath's face. The knuckles of his hand that clasped the Edge Adamantine whitened. "Dare harm even one hair of her, Witch," he shouted hoarsely, "and I'll put this dagger through your heart!"

Avarclon plunged forward as though spurred, climbing swiftly through the air. The White Witch stood unflinching, eyes fixed beyond him, her countenance betraying not the slightest fear. Softly, not to Irrylath, she spoke.

"Harry him."

Instantly her five remaining darkangels broke away from Irrylath's brothers and veered back toward their mistress's keep. In another moment, they were swarming about the prince: baiting, feinting, striking and darting. He kept them at bay with the Edge Adamantine. Aeriel spotted those of Irrylath's brothers who rode wingèd lons hastening to him through the air. Oriencor stood at the casement, watching intently, seeming to take no further interest in the contest of the Lady's army against her own forces below.

The pearl gleamed warm on Aeriel's brow. With a start, she realized that, led by Sabr, the allies had broken free of the Witch's vise at last and cleared a path to the Mere. Under their yellow banner, the Istern and Westron forces were surging toward the black water, dragging barges. Aeriel saw the slender Mariners of the Sea-of-Dust dashing ahead of the rest.

Setting small, light skiffs upon the water, the dark people began to row. If they succeeded in crossing the Mere, Aeriel realized, the Lady's forces could storm the keep. Aeriel's heart quickened—she almost dared to hope. Though badly outnumbered still, the allies were fighting forward again. The tide of battle had begun to turn.

Far to the fore, the skiffs of the dark islanders cut across the oil-smooth Mere. Just as they reached the middle of the lake, Aeriel saw something huge breaking the surface. All at once, the vast black, dull-gleaming head of one of the Witch's water dragons rose from the lake. A moment later, its companion reared beside it, breathing sulfur and smoldering flame. With a roar, the pair of them lunged at the Mariners' skiffs, swallowing half a dozen in the space of a breath.

Aeriel cried out. The formerly tight, orderly fleet of the Mariners drifted, floundering. Seizing another skiff between their jaws, the two dragons tore it asunder, worrying the splinters. Its occupant fell flailing into the poisoned water and disappeared. His fellows hurled javelins, but the mereguints scarcely flinched. Those islanders who tried to row around and on toward the keep, they snapped up and devoured.

Oriencor remained oblivious, eyes fixed above on the battle of Irrylath and his brothers against her icari. Beyond and below, on shore, Pendarlon charged down the beach, scattering a host of the Witch's creatures. With a bound, the lyon of the desert plunged from shore—and did not sink into the flat, reflectionless waters of the Mere. Aeriel swallowed her surprise. The flightless lons could do that, she recalled: run across a fluid or fragile surface without breaking through. A dark rider clung to his radiant mane.

"Erin!" Aeriel cried, recognizing her friend in a rush of euphoria and fear.

Bright Burning hung, still sheathed, at the dark girl's side. *Why?* Aeriel cried inwardly, furious. *Why hasn't she drawn it?* And then the answer came to her, plain as the light of Solstar: *Because the glaive is linked to me. She cannot draw it except when I will.* Aeriel flushed in horrified chagrin. Pendarlon bounded over the black, smooth Mere.

"Draw the sword," Aeriel breathed.

Upon Pendarlon's back, Erin's head snapped up. She cast about her, frowning. Aeriel slapped her own hip, where the sword had once hung. So strong was the connection now, pearl to glaive, that Aeriel half imagined she could feel the sword-belt about her own waist still.

Desperately, she whispered, "Now!"

And a moment later, as the lyon neared the Witch's dragons, the dark girl seized Bright Burning and pulled it from its sheath. The glaive coruscated, ablaze in her hand. Aeriel felt the well-remembered sense of vertigo and, reeling, fought against being drawn into the flame of the blade as, with a savage swipe of the burning sword, Erin slashed the dark, liquid eye of the nearest mereguint as it stooped to seize another of her people's skiffs.

A moment later, Aeriel saw Marelon, the Feathered Serpent of the Sea-of-Dust, breaking the surface of the Mere beside them. Her great vermilion jaws snapping, she twined about the throat of the injured dragon. Their thrashing scarcely disturbed the glass-smooth surface of the Mere. Erin and Pendarlon sprang on as Marelon dragged the mereguint under. Erin brandished her glaive at the other dragon, but it recoiled, diving, and disappeared. Pendarlon roared in fury. The dark girl called out and gestured toward the halls of Winterock. Behind her, the Mariners regathered and rowed.

But how do they mean to enter? Aeriel wondered suddenly. *The keep has no door.* On the shore, the Witch's forces, now gravely disarrayed, were growing ever more ragged. Most of Syllva's people had crowded into the barges now to cross the Mere. Not far from shore, the mudlick, jaws gaping, reared up before the Lady's barge. Syllva shot it through the mouth with an arrow made of silver and gold. Ahead, Erin and Pendarlon had nearly reached the keep.

Without warning, the second mereguint broke the surface of the Mere before them. Its breath smoked, sulfurous yellow. Thundering, the dragon rose, towering over them. With a snarl, the lyon dropped to a crouch. Erin sprang to stand upon his back as, like a black bird, the mereguint's vast head swooped, jaws wide, its teeth each as long as Erin's arm. The dark girl let go of the lyon's mane, taking hold of her blade's hilt in both hands.

"Erin!" Aeriel screamed, reaching out across a hopeless distance—and yet it seemed her own voice echoed in the singing of the blade.

As the dark girl swung the burning sword, Aeriel shut her eyes, feeling a sense of motion and of draining, a sweeping rush as though she herself were circumscribing an arc. Through her own body, she felt the crunch of broken scales, cloven spine, and the waft of something dark and mighty above her collapsing in coils upon coils into the Mere—until gasping, shuddering, Aeriel pulled back, opening her eyes, willing herself away from merger with the sword.

In the lake below, the dead mereguint floated, head severed from its body, black blood iridescent upon the shadowy surface of the Mere. A haze of acrid yellow smoke drifted over it. Not far from it, the lyon, with the dark girl still crouched upon his back, bounded onto the ledge of the castle directly beneath Aeriel. The burning sword blazed in Erin's hand. Drained by even such brief contact with the glaive, Aeriel tottered.

"Erin. Oh, Erin," she breathed.

In the sky overhead, one of Irrylath's brothers

sliced a darkangel with his hooked Istern sword. Oriencor's lip curled in a snarl. Eyes fixed on the battle in the air, she seemed not to have noticed Erin vanquishing her dragons below. Aeriel wondered if the White Witch had even heard her crying the dark girl's name. Above, the prince of Avaric finished off his brother's darkangel with the Edge Adamantine. In silence, like its fellow, the icarus fell.

"Irrylath fights well," Ravenna's daughter murmured, "with great brilliance and passion. I will grant him that. One by one, my darkangels topple."

On the far shore, her troops no longer held any semblance of order. Company by company, her minions were straying to a stop. Absorbed in the aerial battle, Oriencor remained oblivious. A rush of sudden understanding overtook Aeriel. Like an overambitious juggler unable to catch and rethrow all of her many beads, the Witch was allowing her forgotten ground forces to falter. Such numbers, Aeriel realized, must require tremendous concentration to control—and Irrylath's betrayal had clearly shaken her.

"Traitor!" the Witch muttered bitterly. "I never thought he would desert me in the end."

Keep her distracted! Aeriel told herself. Oriencor

could regather her scattered battalions in a moment, if she chose. Desperately, the pale girl searched her mind for something, anything to keep the other's attention from the battle below.

"Yes, my husband has deserted you," she said, throwing into her voice a hard edge of confidence she did not feel. "As the Ancients of Oceanus once deserted you—as did Melkior."

With a hiss, the White Witch turned from the casement, her green eyes blazing. "What do you know of Melkior, you little fool?"

Aeriel's heart quailed beneath the ferociousness of that gaze, but she steeled herself to stand firm, not to flinch. "That he is a halfling, like you," she flung back, using the word she knew would cut. "That he was your friend once, but he turned from you. He served your mother in the end."

"My mother is dead," the White Witch snarled, "and Melkior no more than her clockwork golam. Gears and wires! He is unimportant."

Angrily, she made as if to turn back toward the fray. Aeriel stifled the cry of protest that would betray her as surely as would Oriencor's taking note of events below.

"The Ancients abandoned you as well," Aeriel said quickly. "They refused to take you with them when they left." The Witch's gaze flicked back to

Aeriel, who struggled to maintain her appearance of calm. She must let no hint of what she saw through the casement show on her face. "That is why you hate the world so. The Ancients' going left you prisoner here."

Oriencor glared at Aeriel. "Their leaving me was all my mother's doing—" she started, then stopped herself. Contemptuously, the half-Ancient bowed her white lips in a smile. "But I do not hate the world, little sorceress—though perhaps my mother thought so. I do not care one way or another what happens to the world when I am gone."

Beyond the window, another darkangel fell.

"You are right about the Ancients, though," Oriencor continued evenly. "They broke my heart, leaving me. Soon, however, they will welcome me—they must, for I have proved myself their peer. Have I not labored these thousand years to join them?"

Frowning, Aeriel shook her head, not understanding what the other meant. The White Witch gave a derisive snort. She had turned her attention wholly away from the window now. Hurriedly, Aeriel blanked her features, lest her delight show through. If only she could keep Oriencor occupied a little longer, then the allies had a chance.

"The Ancients will never return here, of course," said the Witch. Her tone grew fierce. "So if I wish to share their company again, it is up to me. Don't you see? I mean to join my peers on Oceanus and claim my birthright there. It is to that end I have been pillaging this planet for a thousand years."

Aeriel stared at her, more baffled than before. *But they're dead,* she thought. Oriencor spoke as though Oceanus were green and blooming still, not ravaged by plagues and horrors. Unexpectedly, Ravenna's daughter smiled her cool, malevolent smile.

"My mother told you nothing of this, I see. So not even she suspected my plans." The White Witch laughed. "Good."

"She said you were killing the world for vengeance—" Aeriel began.

Oriencor nodded curtly. "Oh, I am. In part. At first, many years ago, I longed simply to ruin my mother's work, to force her and her fellows to abandon this world. I hoped they would construct new chariots and take me with them when they returned home."

Distractedly, she stroked the wet windowsill, its odd moisture pooling in the light of sinking Solstar—yet, Aeriel noticed, wherever Oriencor laid her hand, the water thickened, congealing like candlewax.

"But they were very stubborn," the White Witch sighed. "At last I saw I must obtain the means to depart this world myself."

"But you've no chariot...," Aeriel started. Below, Syllva, in the prow of the foremost Istern barge, was halfway to the keep.

"You underestimate me," the White Witch snapped, her back to the scene below. "I have built one: a fiery engine to cross heaven. What did you think I wanted the duaroughs for?"

Aeriel stared. With the pearl's aid, she envisioned the captured duaroughs deep underground —building the Witch her means of escape. The lorelei leaned back, bracing her arms against the frozen windowledge. In the air beyond the window, yet another darkangel plummeted, run through by Irrylath. Below, the Mariners of the islands were clambering onto Winterock's narrow, icy shore. They tried the keep's walls with their weapons, but their spearheads chipped and broke, brittle with the cold. Erin hacked once, experimentally, at the doorless crystal with the blade of the burning sword.

"My fuel is gathered," laughed Oriencor, "though there's so little water on this world, it's taken me a long time to steal enough."

Aeriel could not think what she meant. Water to fuel an engine's fires? Ravenna's daughter smiled thinly.

"Didn't you learn anything in NuRavenna, little sorceress? Water consists of two elements," she said. "One is a fuel, like wax or oil; the other, a vapor that we breathe and that enables fire to burn. My chariot requires both elements in great quantity."

Even as she spoke, the pearl with eerie clarity strung the beads before Aeriel's inner eye so that she was able to picture what Oriencor described: little spots of fire mating and dancing, twining and untwining upon long strands. Impatiently, the White Witch went on.

"And our world's water, unlike that of Oceanus, contains a third component, one that keeps it soluble even in cold shadow. Life-giving to you," the lorelei said, "it is poisonous to my kind."

Aeriel remembered suddenly the bright, hot liquor Talb the Mage had once distilled to poison a darkangel. Oriencor sighed.

"But bind that component—neutralize it—and water grows murky, sluggish, cold."

Aeriel thought of the dark, oil-smooth waters of the Mere below.

"Remove it entirely, and you have winterock."

The Witch's gesture encompassed the whole palace. Behind her, Syllva and the others in barges below drew nearer the castle. Some of the Witch's lesser water-creatures swarmed about the barges, but without their mistress's will to guide them, their attacks had become clumsy and half-hearted. The bowwomen of Isternes picked them off over the barges' rails. Aeriel hardly saw—for she stood gazing at the white, frigid walls around her, open-mouthed in astonishment at her new understanding: *water*. More water than she had ever dreamed, enough to break the whole parched world's drought —if only it were not all of it dead, hardened, transformed into stone! Again she shook her head.

"But...even if you could reach Oceanus—" she started.

"I *will*," Oriencor cut in. "I have the Ancient charts. I know the way."

"But you'll be crushed!" Aeriel exclaimed. "Torn apart. No creature born here can bear the weight of that world."

Oriencor sneered. "Do you really think me the weak and puny thing that once I was?"

Upon the shores of the Mere, Orroto-to, leading her Ma'a-mbai and the other desert tribes, Sabr and her mounted bandits, Irrylath's eldest and youngest brothers, Nar and Hadin, and her own brother Roshka were making short work of the foe. Above, Irrylath and the rest of his brothers closed in on the two remaining icari. Calmly, the White Witch eyed her.

"The gravity of Oceanus might pull *you* to bits, little mortal, but I have found a way to fortify myself against that Ancient tide."

Aeriel frowned, trying desperately to understand. The lorelei smiled a wicked, piercing smile. Suddenly, sickeningly, Aeriel knew what she would say.

"Souls," the White Witch murmured, speaking the word as though it were delicious to her. "Souls to feed me and make me strong. That is all I require now: many sweet, struggling souls. I haven't had nearly enough of them yet."

Aeriel stared, speechless. Beyond the window, another darkangel fell from the air. Below, the Witch's forces were being routed and driven away. Some simply milled upon the shore until picked off by the allied troops not yet in boats.

The White Witch stood laughing at her. Staring into those cold green eyes, Aeriel felt a sudden horrifying suspicion grip her like a vise: it had all been too easy. The Witch *knew*. She had known all along. Deliberately, Oriencor turned back to the casement's view and sighed.

"A fine slaughter."

Shaking, Aeriel gazed down at the battlefield, expecting to see the lorelei's forces regathered in an instant to attack. Yet her monstrous crew remained in utter rout. Only isolated bands of resisters still fought. Directly below, Erin, with broad sweeps of the burning sword, attacked the doorless palace. Its crystal hissed and vaporized at the bright blade's touch.

"You don't," Aeriel stammered, mystified. "You don't seem to *care*."

The Witch glanced at her. "You mean that my troops have been slaughtered? I don't. They were *supposed* to be slaughtered, you little fool. Did you think I would really rely for long on soulless drones to defend me? They're far too much trouble to control."

Stunned, Aeriel felt her heart constricting painfully. It was she who had been the dupe, not Oriencor. Beyond her, in the air, the last, wounded darkangel fled screaming. Irrylath's twin brothers, Syril and Lern, sped in pursuit. Arat, nursing a torn and bleeding shoulder, sat bowed in the saddle, his brother Poratun bending close to examine it. Irrylath turned his gaze toward the Witch's tower. Oriencor pierced Aeriel with green eyes as she laughed.

"Don't you realize this has all been for my pleasure?" she inquired, almost companionably. "I have allowed this battle, this massacre, solely for my delight. Mayhem amuses me. Ah, I see your little friend below us has breached the wall."

Looking down, Aeriel saw Erin cutting a wide entryway into the great doorless palace.

"As soon as they land, your forces will storm the keep," Oriencor said. "But they are not guided and protected, as you were, by Ravenna's pearl, are they?" Her laugh was deep. "Winterock will swallow them. Then they will wander, lost and shivering, for a time—not long—before I go to gather them."

Aeriel recoiled. The Witch's words unnerved her. Desperately, she glanced at the window. How long before the barges landed? Oriencor lilted on.

"Some of them will die before I reach them, which will be a pity—a great waste of souls. But I will have enough. Only the best and the bravest, the hardiest and most fearless of your people will survive long enough for me to sip their lives away."

Aeriel bit her lip, panicked. She had to find a way to stop the Witch before Syllva and her followers reached the keep! Far below, Erin and Pendarlon paced, impatient for the barges. The dark islanders patrolled the thin, icy ledge, driving off the Witch's creatures that occasionally surfaced. Aeriel's thoughts spun. Even if she shouted from the tower, her voice would never be heard above the din of battle. And yet, she must warn them! She felt the warmth of the pearl upon her brow brighten suddenly. All at once, she remembered. Of course. She could speak to Erin through the burning sword.

Aeriel shut her eyes. Ignoring all distraction, she willed herself to make contact, to merge once more with the flame of the blade. A moment later she felt the familiar disorientation, sensed herself being drawn into the sword, her substance drained. Erin's face loomed before her, half an arm's reach away. She felt the motion of the dark girl's stride.

"Aeriel!" her friend gasped, halting. "Where are you?" she cried. "It's been nearly a daymonth—"

"Above you in the tower," Aeriel whispered

urgently. "Listen! Fly for your lives. The castle's a trap! Don't enter—"

An open-hand blow knocked her to the floor.

"Silence! Not another word, you stupid girl," Oriencor snarled.

Half-stunned, Aeriel moaned and blinked back tears. Her cheek stung, numb with cold. The bone of her jaw smarted. Her neck felt wrenched. The White Witch stood over her.

"Did you think I would let you alert them?" she grated. "You are here because it amuses me to let you watch. You will not be allowed to interfere."

Poised, Ravenna's daughter glared down, her green eyes merciless. In another moment, Aeriel was sure she would swoop and throttle her. Beyond her captor, the casement held nothing but distant darkangels and open sky—but through the pearl's link to the sword, Aeriel glimpsed the dark girl's startled look, then saw her turn, crying out to the approaching barges, gesturing them frantically away. Aeriel fought to keep relief and triumph from lighting her face for the Witch to read.

"I will have my souls," Oriencor growled, plainly unaware of what was occurring below. "The very finest, the most *alive,* shall make me strong for my journey across heaven."

Aeriel felt the swordlink flicker. She let it die. It had achieved its end—and cost her much of her remaining strength.

"But they're dust," she protested weakly, drained. "The people of Oceanus died...."

The other laughed. "They *would* have died, long since, if they were mortal like you. But they are not. They are Ancients, and live a very long time."

She still doesn't understand, Aeriel thought wearily, in wonder. *She doesn't know about the plagues and the destruction. She thinks if she goes there, she will find all Oceanus alive.* Then, *If she knew—if I could show her—would she stop?*

"All the Ancients of Oceanus perished," Aeriel managed, speaking as plainly as she knew how, "in a great war dozens of thousands of daymonths ago."

Ravenna's daughter laughed again. "Lies! My mother told you that. It's all nonsense. The Ancients are as gods, *are* gods. And soon I will join their ranks. I have proven myself their equal in sorcery. Soon I will claim the birthright of my Ancient blood and walk at last upon my mother's world."

"There's no one there!" Aeriel searched feverishly for a way to convince her. "Their chariots have long since stopped coming. They no longer speak across the Void."

The White Witch scoffed. "Tired of us. Tired of little minions, little golams, little living toys. Weary—as I am weary—of all the lesser creatures of this world. Weary of you all! Do you think, once I am on Oceanus, that I will deign to return ever again to this place? That I will trouble myself to speak with any of you across the Void?"

"They're dead!" Aeriel insisted, despairing, realizing as she did that it was hopeless. No words she could speak would ever persuade Oriencor.

The bitter savor of the Witch's heart lingered even now upon her tongue. She would have spat, if it could have done any good, but the grains had long since dissolved. She could not get the taste out of her mouth. Ravenna's voice came back to her then, or perhaps it was the pearl's murmuring again: *Crush the Witch's army. Destroy her dark-angels*—and without so much as a jolt of surprise, Aeriel understood why she must give the pearl to Ravenna's daughter.

The Ancient jewel enabled its bearer to separate genuine from illusory. Fiery images of Oceanus's destruction burned bright in Aeriel's mind, with none of the mistiness of possibility and all the unmistakable clarity of fact. Only in claiming the pearl would Oriencor know, beyond all doubt, that Oceanus was dead and the Ancient race no more, that no end could come of killing and abandoning the world. Better to use her vast sorcery to heal it now—it was the only birthright Ravenna's heir would ever know.

Have you ever treasured something, child, a thing so dear you thought you could never give it up—then learned you must? Aeriel understood the Ancient's question now as well, and suddenly all courage failed her. Without the pearl, she would be bereft, robbed forever of its subtle, all-pervading light. It had been a part of her so long that now she could feel its substance in her very bones. Relinquishing it would be like cutting off her own hand, like dying. Doubtless she *would* die—for without the pearl to keep away the cold, she would swiftly freeze.

"Oceanus is dead," she told the other, with all the certainty and conviction at her command. Rising painfully, Aeriel reached to pull the pearl's chain from her hair. "Take this if you do not believe. Take your mother's gift, Oriencor, and behold for yourself."

Her hand shook. Holding out the pearl to the Witch was the hardest thing she had ever done. *Take it,* she wanted to cry. *Take it quickly!* But all at once, she heard a shout. Startled, the pearl still in her hand, Aeriel turned. Avarclon wheeled and thrashed to a halt just outside the broad, high window of the tower. His hooves clattered against the winterock as he flailed and scrambled, unable to hover easily so near the keep. Irrylath leaned forward, clutching the starhorse's mane.

"Aeriel!" he cried. "Aeriel!"

Oriencor turned from the pale girl to sneer at him. "Begone, traitor," she spat. "You and your Horse and your Blade do not frighten me. Aeriel is mine."

"Monster! Lorelei," Irrylath shouted at her. Turning his gaze once more to Aeriel, he cried urgently, "Has she harmed you? Give me your hand."

Avarclon's hooves clashed and rang against the frigid stone. His wings, fanning the air, swept and battered against the tower's outer wall. Irrylath strained forward, reaching his free hand for Aeriel, but he could not get close. The window was not large enough for Avarclon to pass through. Irrylath hacked at the casement relentlessly with the Blade Adamantine. Ignoring him, the White Witch turned away.

"What is it you would give me?" she said contemptuously.

Aeriel gazed back at her. The jewel glimmered in the pale girl's outstretched hand. "That with which your mother entrusted me," she whispered. "The pearl of the soul of the world."

Oriencor tilted her head, eyeing the pearl with new interest. The pale girl nodded.

"Who bears it cannot be fooled by lies."

The other's green eyes studied Aeriel intently suddenly. "Has my mother acknowledged my birthright at last?" she murmured.

"All Ravenna's sorcery is in here," Aeriel told her, "all her knowledge for the running of the world. The making of it cost her life."

Oriencor's eyes grew hungry, bright. "Give it to me, then," she answered, reaching.

"Don't let her touch you!" Irrylath cried. Great chunks of winterock broke and fell away from the Blade. The wall had a gap in it now, still not large enough. Avarclon whinnied and smote with his hooves. "Aeriel," Irrylath insisted. "Come to me. I'll take you away!"

Aeriel looked at him in surprise, at the desperation on his face, the sweat running down from his temples even as his breath burned and steamed like a dragon's in the freezing air. The pearl glowed in her hand.

"It's my inheritance," Oriencor was muttering. "I'll take it with me when I go to Oceanus."

"Aeriel," Irrylath called urgently, leaning once more through the battered window. "Come—answer me!"

If he leans any farther, she thought fearfully, *he'll fall.* His arm stretched out to her, hand open, palm up. A wild longing filled her suddenly as she realized she could go with him. If she went now, she wouldn't die. She could keep the pearl, all its strange sorcery and light—keep it for herself. Irrylath would pluck her away, and they would escape.

"Why do you hesitate?" Oriencor demanded sharply. "Put it into my hand."

Aeriel stared at her, shaking. The Witch was already defeated, all her minions put to flight. *But she has not been redeemed!* a voice rising unbidden within her prodded. *She has not been persuaded that what you say is true. Go with Irrylath, and you will have won a hollow victory. The world will not be healed. The Witch will soon rebuild her power—till you must fight this same battle all over again.* Bitterly, Aeriel realized that she must fulfill Ravenna's task, no matter what the cost.

"Come—Aeriel!" her husband cried.

The pearl burned bright as Solstar in her palm.

Much as she longed to, she could not go with Irrylath. Shaking her head, she whispered, "Fare well."

Oriencor had begun to laugh. Aeriel saw Irrylath gazing at her in desperate incomprehension. Above the other's laughter, the rasp of his own breathing and Avarclon's, the thrash of the starhorse's wings and the clatter of his hooves, surely the prince could not have heard her words. But she saw from his expression that he had read the frame of her lips, the shake of her head.

Too late, he cried out, "No!" as Aeriel tore her eyes away from his, and turned to put the pearl in the White Witch's hand.

FOURTEEN

Flood

∾

THE WHITE WITCH SCREAMED. AERIEL stood frozen, still touching the pearl. She felt something running out of it and into Oriencor, who stood like a statue, immobile, her mouth fallen open to keen one long, high note that went on and on. Those in barges below and on the battlefield beyond stood halted, turned, staring at the keep. Images had begun to play across the surface of the pearl: pestilence and fire—Oceanus destroying itself.

"Dead?" the White Witch screamed. "*Dead?* How can that be? Not dead. Not dead! Poisoned? Plague? How could they destroy themselves?"

Aeriel could not move, could not take her gaze or her hand away from the pearl. Neither, it seemed, could Oriencor, whose chilling cries continued. Dazed, Aeriel realized that though the pearl was imparting certain knowledge of the Ancients' fate, Ravenna's daughter was denying it, refusing to believe. Aeriel shook her head. Her ears rang with the Witch's protests. It had never occurred to her that Oriencor might refuse the gift.

"It was only we, only *we* they caused to war for their pleasure. They can't—they can't be dead! It isn't possible...."

Aeriel felt a stab of sudden fear. She herself had never refused any knowledge she had received through the pearl. She had no idea what would happen to anyone who tried. She had no idea what was happening to Oriencor now. The Witch seemed to be striving to thrust the pearl back into Aeriel's hand. The aroma of Ancient flowers came to her suddenly as a new image gathered itself within the pearl, that of a dusky lady with indigo eyes.

"Daughter," she said quietly, "believe."

Aeriel stared. This image was no misty construct of the future, no vivid memory of the past—it reflected the present: tangible, alive. A living Ravenna gazed at the White Witch from the surface of the pearl.

"No!" the lorelei gasped, recoiling. "I saw your funeral fire—"

The Ancientlady shook her head. "That was only my body, child. Some arts of the Ancients you never learned. My inner essence has been translated, that my messenger might bear me to you. All my being is contained within this pearl. The whole of my magic, my very soul—yours, if you will but accept!"

The White Witch's cries rose to shrills and then to shrieks.

"Never!"

Aeriel would have fled, flung her hands over her ears if only she could have moved. The coldness of the Witch swept over and through her as never before, for the pearl no longer gave her any warmth. Ravenna's image watched her daughter with horror and pain.

"Take it back!" shrieked the Witch. "I do not want your sorcery! I have my own sorcery now...."

Fractures appeared in the winterock around them. By means of the pearl, Aeriel felt the hair-thin cracks running the length of the palace, down below the waterline, below even the bottom of the Mere. She glimpsed the figures trapped in the walls of Winterock stirring, awakening, opening their eyes. The whole keep shifted, shuddering, with a low rumbling that rolled under the high, terrible piercing of the Witch's screams.

"Accept, or you are lost!" Ravenna cried urgently. "Use my gift to heal this world...."

Her image reached out to Oriencor, hands outstretched in appeal. Aeriel was aware of Syllva in her Istern barge below sounding her warhorn, signaling retreat. The dark islanders fled the palace terrace to their skiffs and stroked for the far shore. Erin grasped Pendarlon's mane as he leapt away across the Mere, which had begun to lose its dark opacity. The Witch's creatures writhed and struggled in the lightening waters.

"Believe me, daughter," Ravenna besought her. "My Ancient race and their world are no more."

But Oriencor fought the knowledge of the pearl even now. The palace shuddered again, the floor beneath Aeriel's feet tilting. She heard crashes, like slabs of crystal plunging and shattering.

"It's a lie. A lie—I won't believe it! They can't be dead!"

"Stop," Aeriel tried to tell her. "Stop screaming, or the whole palace will fall."

The other paid her no heed, fingers tightening on the pearl as though she meant to crush it.

"Daughter, turn back—" Ravenna called desperately.

Then the pearl shattered against Aeriel's hand, and the Ancient's image shattered with it, scattering, vanishing. The Witch's webbed fingers bore down upon Aeriel's. She felt the shards of corundum biting into her flesh. A white mist billowed from the broken shell, cloudlike and full of sparkling fire. It filled the room, enveloping them both. Oriencor wrenched around as if trying to tear free of the pearl, batting at the mist and colored sparks as though they ate at her. Aeriel felt nothing but a slight glimmer, an almost-pleasant glow.

She had cut her thumb upon the broken edge of the pearl. Some portion of the billowing light was running into her through the wound. She breathed it in. It alighted on her skin and entered her pores, crept under her fingernails, filled her ears and hair. She felt it, fiercely hot, like burning silver in her blood. She, too, cried out then, not with pain, but with surprise.

"You," Oriencor gasped, turning back to her now. Her tone was a rasp, as though the misty light had seared her lungs. "You! Little sorceress. I curse the day that Irrylath first carried you away, and I curse the hour that ever you came to this keep with your message and your poisonous gift. Undone! All my sorcery undone! By *you,* my mother's catspaw. Your very innocence your shield."

The White Witch was dying, Aeriel realized. For those who could not accept, the knowledge in the pearl was deadly. Even now, her creatures thrashed, perishing in the disenchanted waters below. Aeriel had never dreamed, not for a moment, that the pearl could harm as well as heal.

"I never meant you ill in giving you the pearl," she cried. Nor could she believe that Ravenna had meant her daughter any harm. "I meant only to show you, to ..."

"To make me see?" Oriencor grated, her beautiful bell-like voice now turned to potsherds grinding, to silk rending and metal twisting. "To change me back from what I am into what I was before, a mortal, halfling, Ancient's daughter? Don't you *understand*?"

Winterock shuddered again, and the floor dropped a quarter of an ell before catching itself. The dead creatures in the lake below were dissolving into noxious mist. The palace shook like something struggling to awake. Both Oriencor and Aeriel staggered, but neither could release the broken, billowing pearl.

"Don't you see?" Oriencor shrilled. "I am no more redeemable than one of my darkangels—one of my *true* darkangels. For I am not incomplete, as Irrylath was when you rescued him. I have eaten hearts and drunk blood and drunk *souls*. My heart is dust. I could not return to what I was even if I wished—*and I do not wish it!* I want to walk among my peers—I want the Ancients alive on Oceanus, and I curse you for taking the hope of that—my only purpose—away."

Her last words were a scream that rent the palace from tower to base. The shock threw Aeriel to her knees. By means of the pearl, she was aware of the now-transparent waters of the Mere pouring into the breaches. She thought of the duaroughs held prisoner in the depths of the palace below and hoped desperately for their deliverance.

"Aeriel! Aeriel!"

Above the din, someone was crying her name, had been crying her name frantically for some time. She turned to see Avarclon bearing Irrylath away from the crumbling palace. Great chunks of winterock sheared off and hurtled down. The prince sat helpless, unable to turn his unbridled steed. Without bit or reins, Irrylath could not compel the Avarclon to wheel and bear him back to Aeriel.

A snarl brought her sharp around. Oriencor was still on her feet, though barely. Her gown was in tatters, her once-white skin, now ashen, was flaking and falling away like curls of burnt paper. Her hair, a nest of tiny, filament-thin snakes, streamed and billowed in a wind Aeriel could not feel. Aeriel shrieked and shrank back even as the Witch's green eyes pinned her.

"I'll have you," she whispered, her ruined voice soft as gravel crushing against itself. "You've destroyed me, but I'll see you undone before me. I'll have your heart, your eyes. Little sorceress, I'll have your soul!"

She reached out one dagger-nailed hand as Aeriel screamed, trying frantically to pull free. Above her in the air, a long way off, she heard Irrylath cry out as well. The White Witch's hand darted toward her. Aeriel shrank, straining, leaned desperately away. She felt Oriencor's talons barely brush her closed eyelids—not enough even to break the skin, but enough to send their cold through her like a knife.

All the light in the world went out. Setting Solstar vanished. Then Aeriel felt the Witch's hand, still holding hers to the broken pearl, fall away into ashes, into dust—just as the palace shuddered for the final time and plunged inexorably down, down toward the roiling Mere below.

WINTEROCK WAS FALLING, BUT IT WAS no longer made of stone. All Oriencor's enchantments must have unraveled at her death, Aeriel thought, almost calmly, as she fell. Water thundered all around her. She could not see, could not breathe, heard only the water's roaring. The pearl-stuff in her blood told her a little of what was happening around her. She wondered when she would reach the hard end of her fall and die.

But no end came. The rushing and buffeting went on and on. After an eternity, she realized that though she was falling still, she was no longer plunging straight downward. *The palace has collapsed into the lake:* the knowledge came to her with eerie clarity. *You are being borne along beneath the surface now.*

She had no air left in her lungs. The cage of her ribs ached, burning, bursting. *Just a while longer,* she told herself. *Hold out a little longer—* though there hardly seemed any point. She could not swim. Deep below the surface of the Mere, water all around, she was keenly aware that as soon as she opened her mouth and drew breath, she would perish.

Perhaps she would faint first and know nothing of dying. Drowning was not such a terrible end after all, she told herself. She'd always feared it, ever since slipping into a cave pool as a child and being pulled, sick and sputtering, onto the bank by her mistress Eoduin. But there was no bank here and no companion to rescue her.

Her head pounded with the lack of air. Presently she would stop fighting, open her mouth and breathe deep of the pummeling torrent. Then she would be dead. *At least the White Witch is dead, too,* she thought drowsily, *and the world is free of her.* The pearlstuff in her blood gave her the certain knowledge of it but could bring her no comfort.

She felt only a crushing sense of failure. She had not fulfilled Ravenna's charge, had not succeeded in converting Oriencor to good. The world would know a brief respite now. But without Ravenna's sorcery, could it ever heal? The pearl was broken, its contents scattered, lost. Still she clung to life, continued to resist the flood. Her own tenacity surprised her. *Stop fighting,* she told herself, preparing to die. *You've failed.*

Someone caught her by the hair, pulled her close across the current. The tremendous buffeting all around them had lessened now. It had become

a fierce undertow, no longer any downward motion to it. Her companion guided her face to his,
put his mouth to hers and gave her breath. Aeriel
clutched at his shirt and clung there, drinking in
the sweet, magnificent air.

Her head cleared, and suddenly she was fighting again, struggling for breath. The other did not
let her break away, did not let her breathe in the
white waters of the Mere, much as she wanted to.
Air! She needed air. Darkness was everywhere.
The icy touch of the Witch's fingers had banished
her sight. Her eyes felt useless, frozen, like orbs
of winterock.

She could not see who it was that held her. But
she felt the strength of his arm around her, his
legs stroking for the surface. She was being borne
upward against the current's tow by someone.
Someone who swam like a fish. Someone who had
been raised by a lorelei. Someone who had swum
the Mere every day of his life for ten long years:
Irrylath.

IT SEEMED AN AGE BEFORE THEY BROKE
the surface. She gasped the sweet air, but weakly
now, half-swooned. Hardly any strength remained
in her limbs. She was content to lie unresisting in
her husband's arms and let the torrent bear them

along. *Miles and miles,* she thought dreamily: the flood must be taking them leagues from where the Witch's palace had once stood. Were the others—those in the barges and upon the shore—safe? She could only hope, wrapped in a darkness devoid of Solstarlight, or Oceanuslight, or stars. Head pillowed on Irrylath's breast, she slept.

Awareness returned to her just as gradually. Water no longer surrounded them. She no longer felt the rush bearing her along. They had stopped moving. Bruised and waterlogged, she felt herself lying on firm ground, stable and solid, if very soggy. Her garment was sopping, and half her hair—she could feel by the gentle give and tug—lay in water. Someone was speaking her name.

She opened her eyes, though without hope of seeing anything. They ached, painfully cold. Then something struck one of them, a hot, stinging drop. Another fell upon her brow, then ran burning and salt into her other eye. She flinched, blinking, and became aware of stars overhead, a blaze of them. Someone was bending over her.

"Aeriel, Aeriel," he said.

She moaned and, moving, realized how stiff she was. The pearlstuff in her blood made her feel hazy and strange.

"Irrylath," she muttered, reaching for him. "I was drowning, and you came for me."

To have rescued her, she realized, he must have dived from Avarclon's back. Her dream returned to her, clear at last: Irrylath plunging headlong from high above into the roiling confusion of the flood below. The starhorse had been trying to bear him to safety, carry him up and away, but he had refused to be saved without her, had come after her instead. Not fallen. Dived. Irrylath clasped her to him.

"Oriencor is dead," he whispered. "You killed her, and the palace fell."

She felt him shudder. His tears ran onto her cheek and forehead. Blinking the burning drops from her eyes, she saw mud flats stretching all around, black soil fanning out on every hand. Water lay in sheets, a cool misty smoke rising from it in wraithlike clouds. Broken bits of furniture, tapestry, devices lay scattered about them like a shipwreck.

Her wedding sari, yellow and immune to any moisture, tangled in a patch of scrub nearby. The mist, full of colored sparks still, swirled and drifted, at times obscuring the sky. Oceanus hung canted in heaven amid a fiery swirl of stars.

Strangely, the night did not feel cold. At last, Irrylath drew back from her.

"Not I," he said. "Not I, but you—*you* killed her."

She had never been so close to him before. Even by starlight, she saw the four long scars that raked one side of his face, and the fifth that trailed just below the jaw. The scars Pendarlon had given him, an age—no, only two years—ago, when he had been a half-darkangel in Avaric. She laid her hand along those scars.

"In Winterock," she said, "while the palace stood, the pearl gave me a glimpse of what the White Witch did to you."

She saw him flinch, felt the shock that passed through him. He gazed at her. "I thought you knew all along," he whispered. "I thought your green eyes saw everything."

She shook her head. Was that why he had stayed away—shunning not her, but the things he feared she knew?

"It's why I thought I wanted Sabr," he said, "because she knows nothing of that, and even if she ever learns, she'll not believe it. She'll insist on thinking I was brave."

"You were brave," said Aeriel. She remembered

him leading the battle from Avarclon's back, swooping to rescue Sabr, confronting his own and his brothers' darkangels. "You are the bravest one I know."

Irrylath shook his head. "I wasn't. I'm not. Oriencor found my every flaw. In the end, she broke me like a toy."

"And you imagined I might do the same?" Aeriel mused, stung, full of wonder at her own stupidity. Blind! Until this moment, she had been blind. "So you turned to Sabr, who adores you— lonely for someone who did not know your past, longing only to escape that painful memory."

She saw the prince's jaw set, as he nodded, thinking of the Witch. His eyes were like two lampflames burning.

"But Oriencor is dead now," he whispered fiercely. "I will never dream of her or feel her touch or hear her voice again. My rescuer. You have delivered me."

She wanted to contradict him, to protest: he had turned away from Oriencor of his own volition, striking her seventh son from the air long before Aeriel had handed her the pearl. But all she did was put her lips to his to make him still. The night was a blaze of Oceanuslight and stars. The mist swirled around them in whispers, like wraiths.

Scattered sparks still drifted randomly, alighting in Irrylath's hair. Her husband put his arms about her, drew her to him like a man so long dying of thirst he almost feared to drink.

Then something with a human shape but made all of golden light glided past them and vanished into the mist. Aeriel started back from the prince with a cry. The first apparition was gone, but a moment later, from another quarter, a different figure strode by—again of golden light—this one a young man, garbed in a style she did not recognize. He might have glanced at them before disappearing into the fog. Aeriel felt Irrylath's arms about her tighten.

"What are they?" she gasped.

"Souls," he whispered. "All the souls Oriencor or her darkangels ever captured or drank. All those she kept prisoner in the walls of Winterock. Delivered now. Look. The air is full of them."

Aeriel gazed upward, following the line of his arm. The sky above shimmered with revenants of golden light, ascending toward deep heaven. They seemed to add to the number of the stars. The mist and the night were lit by them. The air felt heavy and electrified. The hair on Aeriel's arms and along the nape of her neck stood on end. She held on to Irrylath.

"They mean us no harm," he murmured, then stopped himself, shivering. "At least, they mean *you* no harm. You freed them."

A luminous figure resembling a woman of Zambul came to a halt not ten paces from them. The sparkling fog swirled and thickened all around. As the spirit gazed at them, the corners of her mouth turned up ever so slightly in the beginning of a smile. Then she lifted her arms and arose, right in front of them, elongating and attenuating as she ascended.

The mist closed denser and denser before lifting suddenly without dissipating. Gazing upward, Aeriel saw that the stars were now completely obscured. She could no longer see the confluence of souls ascending, caught only glimmers of them in the distance, like flashes of light. The electrical quality of the air intensified. She heard a long, low rumble she could not identify. More flashes. Another rumbling. Something wet and cold struck her skin.

She flinched in surprise, felt Irrylath do the same. The shock repeated itself: a spattering of droplets. The scent of water pervaded the air. The pattering drops grew larger and more numerous. They began to fall harder, more steadily. A wet breeze rose and slapped at them. The sensation was cold, thrilling, strange. She huddled against the shelter of Irrylath's body. The sound of falling water drummed against the night, marked by low booming and glimmers of light.

"What is it?" she exclaimed.

"Water from heaven," he answered wonderingly, holding out one hand to catch the falling drops. "Such as fell in Ancient times—a dozen thousand daymonths past."

The water came in wind-whipped spatters now, gusting and unabating. Aeriel cupped her own hands and brought them to her lips. The taste was cool and sweet, full of air and minerals. She held her joined palms up to Irrylath and let him, too, drink. Still clasping her to him, he kissed her hands.

"The drought of the White Witch is broken," he told her. "It's rain."

FIFTEEN

Rime's End

AERIEL. AERIEL, AWAKE, A STILL, IN-
ward voice whispered. The pale girl shifted, doz-
ing. Her husband lay sleeping beside her, his
breaths even and deep. The strange pattering of
rain drummed lightly now. Their makeshift tent
rustled gently with the soft, constant wind. Aeriel
pressed closer to Irrylath, too drowsy to listen to
any sounds but these.

After the flood, Irrylath had made them this
small pavilion out of her wedding sari. Gathering
poles from the surrounding flotsam, he had set
them upright in the soft ground, then draped and
wound the yards and yards of yellow stuff about
their frame. The magical air-thin cloth kept out
the damp. Their clothing dried quickly, and the

ground over which their shelter stood soon, inexplicably, became dry.

The quiet murmur came again: *Aeriel, awake.* Still half-dozing, she forgot it the moment she opened her eyes. Pillowing her head on one arm, she gazed at Irrylath. For the first time since she had known him, his face was at rest—no longer troubled by the Witch's dreams. Smiling now, she remembered the heat of his body these few hours past: what she had hungered for all these daymonths, ever since their marriage day.

"No longer my husband only in name," she murmured, kissing him as she reached to pull a few stray strands of hair back from his lyon-scored face.

Irrylath shifted, sighing, deeply asleep. He never roused. Only a little while ago, he had clasped her to him with such urgency and passion—as though some intervention loomed to part them, as though only a little time remained. Aeriel laughed, amazed at her own unaccustomed happiness. Here beneath their wedding silk, she gazed at her husband with the greatest attention, a lover's gaze. Every inch of him was beautiful to her.

Aeriel. The soft utterance came again, more insistently. Aeriel sat up with a start. She cast about

her, baffled, but she and Irrylath were alone. The
voice—eerily familiar—seemed to come from the
air.

"Where are you?" she whispered.

Here, the answer came. *Within. I am within you
now.*

Aeriel felt a tremor, something stirring in her
blood. The scent came to her suddenly of Ancient
flowers, dusky and sweet. Astonishment washed
over her. She knew the voice.

"Ravenna," she breathed, shaken. When the
pearl had shattered in Oriencor's hand, Aeriel had
thought the Ancientlady—surely then if not before—utterly destroyed.

The still, inward voice seemed to chuckle.
Hardly the whole of what Ravenna comprised, it
murmured, *but a little of her, yes. Call me Ravenna,
if you will: I am part of what she was.*

Aeriel struggled to catch her breath, to take it
in. Overwhelming remorse seized her suddenly.

Why do you sorrow? Ravenna within her asked.
The war is won.

Aeriel's breast heaved, but it was with dry sobs
only. She felt the white marks in the shape of stars
left upon her eyelids by the Witch's touch.

"Because I have failed you," she whispered,

"and all the world. What matter that the war is won, if all the world is lost?"

Lost? the voice of the pearlstuff in her blood exclaimed. *My daughter's evil is at an end, child— her drought broken, her creatures drowned—and all my rime has come to pass....*

"Except the last!" Aeriel exclaimed. Their shelter sighed in the gentle breeze. She gazed about her at the walls of silk, at their scattered garments, at Irrylath. Despair tasted like wormwood in her mouth. "The last line of the prophecy is not fulfilled. Your gift is scattered to the winds. No daughter remains to heal the world and claim the crown. All's lost."

Not lost, the Ancient's voice within her whispered. *It need not be lost.*

Aeriel shook her head. How many more generations had this vast war won for the planet—a handful? A score? So pitifully few it scarcely mattered. Without Ravenna's daughter to guide the healing of the world, Aeriel thought bitterly, everything she and Irrylath had struggled for was vainglory. In the face of the all-devouring entropy, it would all wind down to nothing in the end.

That need not be, the inner voice murmured,

and Aeriel realized belatedly that the pearlstuff in her blood could read her thoughts whether or not she spoke them aloud. *The entropy need not prevail. Another might gather my scattered sorcery and heal the world in Oriencor's stead.*

Aeriel blinked. Her own white radiance lit the enclosed space softly.

"I don't know what you mean," she breathed.

Be my successor, child, Ravenna's voice whispered. *A little of my power is in you now, enough to guide you in gathering the rest.*

"But," she protested, dazed, "I'm not your daughter. The rime says—"

Are you not? the other asked gently. *Did I not tell you in NuRavenna that you and many others of your young race are descendants of my Ancient one, many generations removed? The world is yours now: your birthright, your inheritance. We Ancients are no more. Become my daughter even as Irrylath was once the Witch's son. Accept the crown of the world's heir, Aeriel. I've no one left but you.*

Aeriel sat silent, unable to take it in, to fathom it. "I can't...," she stammered. "I don't know how."

You underestimate yourself. Enough of me remains to show you how to start. It will be a long and mighty task, but not beyond you—with my aid.

Vistas unfolded before her, misty with possibility still: Ravenna's sorcery reclaimed and the world made whole again. Aeriel blinked in surprise, beholding, until she realized that the view came to her through the remnants of the pearl.

But we must haste, the still, quiet voice urged her. *Better to go at once, while still he sleeps.*

The pale girl frowned, gazing at Irrylath. "Go?"

The pearlstuff in her blood swirled restlessly. *Yes. Have you not understood what I have been telling you? This task will consume you. You must leave all else behind.*

Aeriel drew back, a chill breathing through her. "Leave Irrylath?" she cried.

The voice within her subsided. At last it said, *At times we all must give up what we hold most dear for the greater good. I gave up my daughter, all my sorcery, my very life—*

"But Irrylath is my husband," Aeriel exclaimed. "We've only just found one another...."

The whole world needs you, Aeriel, the pearl's voice answered sadly. *And he is only one man.*

New images unfolded before her mind's eye: the planet dying.

"No," Aeriel whispered, "no!"

Anguish racked her. She wished that she might

turn away, ignore the knowledge, refuse the gift—
but the Ancient sorcery was already inside her,
and there was nowhere she might turn.

"Irrylath needs me!" she tried desperately.

I am truly sorry, the pearl's voice murmured,
*but I have allowed you even these brief hours together
at great cost. Time presses. You must not ask more.*

Aeriel gazed down at her prince. Gently, she
cupped his chin in her hand and, still deeply sleeping, he turned his face as though to seek her touch.
An unutterable weight descended upon her. Her
breast felt heavy and sore, and she tasted the
Witch's heart upon her tongue. Aeriel cradled her
husband's cheek, unwilling to let him go.

"He saved me," she whispered, remembering
her terror of the flood. "I can't swim. I'd have
drowned when the palace fell if he had not ..."

Drowned? the voice in her blood exclaimed.
*Nonsense, child. You can't drown. This new body I
gave you is not so easily destroyed.*

A thin thread of cold wound through Aeriel. She
shivered hard. "What do you mean?" she asked,
baffled. "What new body—I don't understand."

The pin, child, the pearl's voice insisted. *Did
you not guess? The White Witch fashioned it so that
it could not be removed without killing you.*

Aeriel's eyes widened. Her free hand flew to the place behind her ear where the pin had been. She felt no soreness there, no scar. "But you plucked it out," she gasped. "You pulled it free—"

Yes, and most of you perished in the flash. I had to rebuild the greater part—though I saved all that I could: your heart, your eyes. Your mind and soul, of course.

With a strangled cry, Aeriel snatched her hand from the sleeping prince's cheek, recoiling in horror—not of him, but of herself. In numb dismay, she stared at the body into which she had awakened feeling so strangely *new*, in the City of Crystalglass, daymonths ago.

"What thing have you made of me?" she gasped. Her eyes returned to Irrylath. He had been a demon once, in Avaric, and she had made him mortal again. She herself had been mortal then—but what was she now? "A monster...," she choked.

No more a monster than the starhorse, Ravenna within her replied, *or any other of my lons. No more than Melkior.*

"A golam," the pale girl managed, shuddering.

Yes.

"A clockwork automaton—like the duarough's underground machines...!"

No. Never. A biological construct. You are still flesh, child, not gears and wire.

Staring at herself, Aeriel laughed weakly, dismayed. "A fine match," she repeated softly, thinking of the starhorse, "this new engine for my soul."

She moved her fingers, clenching and opening her hand—but the motion had become accustomed now, no longer felt odd. Something slid along her arm: a tiny chain, scant as spider's silk—so fine she had not noticed it before. She recognized the filament Ravenna had used to fasten the pearl to her brow. It had become entwined about her wrist somehow—when she had handed the pearl to Oriencor? Distracted, Aeriel shook her head, still staring at her strange, new flesh.

"As like my old form as like ..."

The words trailed away.

It is the soul that makes us human, not the flesh. Believe me, child, if I had had another choice—

"Why did you not tell me?" Aeriel grated furiously. She sat gasping, scarcely able to speak. Outrage and a crushing sense of betrayal strangled her voice.

I did not think that wise, the song in her blood

answered deftly, dispassionately. *I had to conceal my design from your adversary at all costs. If the Witch had read even a glimpse of it in your eyes or so much as suspected what it was you carried, she'd have destroyed you long before you could give her the pearl.*

Aeriel shook her head. Oriencor's words came back to her: *Little fool...no more than her clockwork golam...unimportant!* Slowly, realization dawned. To Ravenna within her, she said at last, "You meant to sacrifice me—our entire army— to that end if need be."

A weary silence.

She was my daughter, Aeriel. I had to try.

No sound in the tent then but night wind's gentle gusting and Irrylath's soft, even breaths. The voice of the pearl said no more for a time.

"I've been your catspaw all along," Aeriel said quietly, amazed. "We have all been your gaming beads." Then, suddenly, sharply, "Did you know the pearl would destroy her when I put it into her hand?"

The pearlstuff within her roused sluggishly, as if reluctantly, seemed to sigh. *I greatly feared it, if she would not accept the gift.*

"And now you would make me the world's heir in place of Oriencor."

She worried the fine, weightless chain about her wrist, but it would neither break nor slip free.

" 'Ravenna's daughter,' " she said bitterly. "Some called me that even before this war. And 'green-eyed enchantress.' " She felt the pearlstuff moving in her blood and shivered. "Perhaps those titles have a grain of truth to them now, after all."

Behold.

Aeriel felt a change within her. Her vision sharpened, becoming infinitely more keen. Everything around her resolved into little burning filaments that twined and juggled, mated and danced. Her own hand, Irrylath, the Edge Adamantine— everything was made of them: strung together from beads of fire.

The stuff of all the world, the voice within her said. These *are my gaming beads. Return to Nu-Ravenna, wearing the crown as my heir, and I will teach you the juggling of them, the spinning and weaving of their strands. You will become a mighty sorceress, Aeriel.*

The pale girl sat gazing at the sleeping prince beside her. She shook her head. "I don't want your sorcery," she whispered. "I want to remain with Irrylath."

The pearlstuff in her blood began to simmer

and seethe. Once again the images of the encroaching entropy flooded her mind.

You must leave him, the Ancient's voice persisted. *The task awaiting you brooks no distraction. You will be far too busy in NuRavenna for such mundane cares.*

Aeriel leaned back and longed to weep. Her eyes stung, but no tears would fall. Despair overwhelmed her. Undeniable as the chain, everything the Ravenna within told her was true.

Child, you are not mortal anymore. Irrylath deserves a bride who will age with him.

The Ancient's words were full of compassion and sorrow, but some stubborn part of Aeriel refused to give in.

"I am his bride," she whispered.

You drank your wedding toast to a half-darkangel in Avaric, Ravenna within her answered gently. *One who meant to kill you in the next hour. But you overcame him with the help of Talb the Mage. The one you wed no longer exists! Irrylath is a man again; the darkangel is no more.*

"He lives!" cried Aeriel. "My own heart beats within his breast."

Because his heart was plucked from him unawares, while he lay helpless beneath the Mage's spell. Don't

*you see, child? Irrylath is bound to you whether he
would or no. Did you not once yourself hear him say
he would turn to Sabr if only he were free?*

"No," Aeriel whispered, resisting still. "He
would not—it's *me* he loves now...." But the
words trailed away. Doubt gnawed at her. Gazing
at Irrylath, she began to fear all his late passion,
all his love were but the outcome of a stolen heart
and Talb the Mage's spell. Aeriel groaned. "But
he is my husband. He's *mine*."

*Are you like the Witch, then, devoid of true love?
Do you want only to possess him?*

"No!" The misery that gripped her was almost
unbearable.

Then set him free.

Silence.

Come, Ravenna's voice reasoned. *You have freed
the wraiths that were the darkangel's brides, and my
lons that had been made into gargoyles. You have
freed the whole world from my daughter's power. Will
you not give Irrylath his freedom now?*

Aeriel sat shaking, frozen. Ravenna's exhorta-
tion filled her with terror. If she gave Irrylath back
his heart, would he be lost to her? She could not
bear the thought—and yet, now that the seed of
suspicion was planted, it seemed she could do

nothing to check its growth. Cold certainty crystallized in her: once freed, he would choose Sabr. The fine chain chafed against her wrist. The pearl-stuff in her blood waited, whispering. Her gaze fell upon the white gown into which she had awakened in NuRavenna.

"I know now what is the fabric of this garment you gave me," she said softly. It felt unspeakably heavy, a great burden in her hand. She did not want to don it again. "Duty."

Sacrifice.

One of the panels of the tiny pavilion was very slightly agape, where two layers of the yellow wedding sari did not quite overlap. Aeriel gazed out through the crack into the night beyond. The rain had long since ceased, the mist beginning to blow away. The star-strewn vault of heaven peered darkly through the grey-white wisps of cloud.

If you lose much, think what you and the world will gain. And others have lost still more. Consider all my former might, reduced now to a scatter of firebeads on the wind and a murmur in your blood.

Aeriel's gaze returned to Irrylath. "This task you would hand me will stretch far beyond the life of any mortal man."

Doubtless. And time presses even now. My sorcery scatters wider with every passing hour. You must begin to gather it, and soon.

The pale girl laughed painfully. What could that matter, without Irrylath? She thought of the task stretching before her, uncountably vast, and herself going companionless through all the years. Loneliness nearly overwhelmed her. Even the Ancientlady Ravenna had had Melkior. Heavily, she sighed.

"Must I never see Irrylath again?"

The Ancient's voice was full of regret. *I fear not. Have you forgot?—Irrylath belongs to the Avarclon.*

Aeriel sat upright with a jolt. Memory filled her of the pact he had struck with the newly awakened starhorse in Isternes: a truce between them and the wingèd Warhorse for his steed until the Witch was overthrown. Aeriel bit back a gasp. She had forgotten that pact, put it wholly from her mind until this moment. All debate would prove meaningless if the starhorse demanded the prince's death in payment for his own.

I built my lons to be just, not merciful, the Ancient voice within her sadly said. *In truth, it was this I meant to spare you when I warned you away in haste.*

The pale girl's hand upon her sleeping husband tightened. "No," she whispered. "No. Tell me what I may do...."

To save him, she meant, but the pearlstuff in her blood spoke before she could finish the thought.

We have come to the rime's end, child. I can only advise. I cannot compel. The choice lies before you: Irrylath or the world. Choose.

Aeriel struggled, fighting for breath. It was hard to speak, the words hurt so. At last she whispered, "If I must give up Irrylath to the vengeance of the Avarclon, then let him at least go as his own man, free."

Her hand shook, but she felt the pearlstuff within her steady it. Sheathed upon the prince's sash, the Blade Adamantine glimmered. Aeriel reached to pull it free. Laying her hand on Irrylath's breast, she drew the white gleaming edge down the center of his breastbone and found her own living heart beneath, placed there two twelvemonths past upon their marriage night. Lost in sleep, the young man never stirred. The edge of adamant held no sting.

Turning the blade to her own breast, she delved and found Irrylath's beating heart, which she had worn these last two years. The pearlstuff pervaded her, sustaining her. No blood spilled from the bright Blade's keen and burning edge. She felt only warmth hot as white Solstar. Taking her own heart from Irrylath's breast, she returned his to its place. With a motion of her hand, she closed the flesh. Then she set her own heart back in her breast and sealed the breach. No mark or scar betrayed what she had done.

"Already," she murmured to Ravenna within, "you have made me a sorceress."

Adamantine glowed bright without a stain, throwing shadows through the little pavilion. One lay now across Irrylath's face. Aeriel herself cast no shadow anymore. Unable even to weep, she turned and set the Blade back in its sheath. Voices sounded in the distance outside the pavilion. Aeriel lifted her head, listening. The prince beside her murmured, shifted, stirred. The voices sounded closer, clearer now.

"Survivors, surely!" A young man's voice. It sounded like her own brother Roshka's.

"By all the underpaths," another cried, one Aeriel had not heard in far too long: Talb the Mage. "Let it be they! The fabric of that pavilion can only be hers."

"Hollo! Hollo!"

Irrylath beside her sat up with a start. Hurriedly, she reached for Ravenna's gown, but her husband caught her hand and brought it to his lips. Without a thought, she caressed his cheek—then she remembered he did not belong to her anymore, and froze. Other voices hailed them from without. Aeriel heard the high, ululating trill that was the greeting cry of the desert wanderers. The prince's head turned in surprise.

"Someone comes," he murmured.

Sick at heart, Aeriel pulled free of him and turned away. His touch was torture to her now. She could not bear to look into his eyes, to see his feelings change as soon as he realized his heart was once again his own. She donned the Ancient's weighty gown. Beside her, the prince caught up his own garments. As he knotted the sash about his waist, he reached to draw her to him again. Aeriel shrank from him. Shaking, she rose to fold the flap of their tent aside and step out to meet the ones who came.

SIXTEEN

Crowns

∾

SPREAD OUT OVER THE VAST BLACK PLAIN
moved a great band of people, combing for survivors or the perished, Aeriel guessed. After the
rain, the mudflats were beginning to drain. A tiny
frog, pale rose, sprang away from her tread with
a jewellike chirp. A damselfly with lacelike wings
darted past her ear. Little shoots of frost green
had sprung up everywhere. Silvery minnows and
other fry swarmed the tiny pools. Gazing at them,
both creature and leaf, Aeriel understood for the
first time how they interlocked, like beads in a
tapestry, each dependent upon the others for its
niche in the greater scheme. The pearlstuff stirred
and whispered in her blood.

"This will never be a Wasteland again," she
murmured full of wonder, "but a fertile marsh."

Catching sight of her emerging from the tent, the searchers hurried toward her with great glad cries. Irrylath's mother, the Lady Syllva, led them, flanked by her bowwomen. The lons of Avaric and elsewhere dotted their ranks. Aeriel spotted others: the chieftess Orroto-to and her desert wanderers, the dark islanders of the Sea-of-Dust. Erin stood beside Pendarlon upon the verges of her people. The Sword hung sheathed and burning at her side. Elation rose in Aeriel, strong as a well-spring, to find the dark girl safe.

Irrylath ducked through the entryway to stand half a pace behind her as the others neared. His brothers gave a triumphant shout. Sabr, heading her cavalry along the party's near flank, looked on, her proud and somber countenance lifting with joy at the sight of him. Aeriel felt her heart constrict, struck suddenly how nearly the face of the prince's cousin resembled his own: Irrylath as he might have looked without scars. Aeriel dared not turn to see how her husband returned the queen of Avaric's gaze.

Drawing close, the others halted before Aeriel. Her brother Roshka stood near the head of the band, Talb the Mage at his side. She felt a momentary surprise to see the Lady's mage above-ground without a daycloak, before she remembered that since nightshade had fallen, he was safe from Solstar's glare. The duarough wizard hobbled toward her across the drying ground.

"So, dear child," he exclaimed, "you are alive, as we had not dared hope, and Prince Irrylath is with you."

She felt the prince's arm slip around her then and tensed, longing desperately both to lean back into his embrace and to draw away—for it could not last. She held herself erect, wondering how soon he would release her and turn to Sabr.

"Yes, we are safe," she managed, to Talb. "How is it, little mage, that I never saw you among the others in battle?" His cloak of obscurity might hide him from the light of Solstar, but surely never from the sight of the pearl.

The other smiled. "I was occupied belowground, aiding my fellows, the free duaroughs, in the rescue of our folk."

Aeriel nodded. "And those aboveground," she asked, lifting her gaze. "How is it so many are come alive through the flood?"

Hadin, the Lady's youngestborn, answered. "Most were already aboard the barges when the palace fell, and the lons saved many of the rest. Marelon alone rescued scores upon scores."

Aeriel spotted the great coils of the plumed,

vermilion serpent far away toward the rear of the company. The lithe lon of the Sea-of-Dust bowed to her. Nearer to hand, Roshka joined his cousin Hadin, laying one hand upon his battle companion's arm.

"Nevertheless, we have been dozens of hours finding one another again."

Aeriel felt the pearlstuff within her blood begin to surge, the white radiance of her skin brightening. Unsure of the effect this inner pearlfire would have on any whom it touched, she laid her hand upon Irrylath's wrist, meaning to thrust him away—but, misinterpreting, he took her hand. She stiffened, recalling in alarm the scathing flame of Erin's sword, but he seemed to suffer no ill. The Lady Syllva gazed at them.

"Children, are you well?" she asked, brow furrowed with concern.

"Truly well, mother," the prince replied. "The war is over, and it is won."

The crowd shifted suddenly, parting and drawing aside. Aeriel saw Avarclon coming forward, tossing his long silvery mane. His nostrils flared wide as he snorted, his pale eyes intent and hard. His hooves rang like cymbals upon the stones embedded in the soft, black silt.

"Indeed, Prince, the battle is done," the

Warhorse said. "But there is yet our bargain to be kept."

Aeriel paled, her hand in Irrylath's growing cold. Had he, too, put the anticipation of this moment from his mind, just as she herself had done? Avarclon had not. How could a lon forget or forgive his own death at the hands of a darkangel—one that, as a mortal boy, had once been his dearest friend?

She saw apprehension flood the Lady Syllva's face as well. The prince's brothers shifted, murmuring. Erin muttered something urgently to Pendarlon, but the lyon shook his mane. Sabr cast about wildly, hand at her knife hilt. Aeriel felt her husband's arm about her tighten, and for a moment, she allowed herself to rest against him before he turned her in his arms.

"Forgive me," he whispered, "for not reminding you that this end must come. I wanted you to think of me alone, these brief hours past, since we had so little time."

His eyes searched hers. The scars on his cheek were full of shadow and light. When he kissed her, the taste of him was so sweet she wanted never to stop. The pearlstuff in her blood flared, as if in warning, but she clung to him, heedless, unwilling to let him go, until at last he pulled free and told her softly, "Fare well."

Turning, he went to kneel before the wingèd horse. The lon of Avaric whickered, stamped. His great grey wings beat, fanning the air. The prince faced him unwavering.

"What you say is true," he replied. "I have a debt to you."

His voice was steady, calm, shaded only with regret and not a trace of fear. The Avarclon shook himself, sidling. His long tail lashed.

"As a darkangel, I ended your life," Irrylath told him. "Yet once the priestesses of Isternes had brought you into the world again, you made yourself my steed and bore me bravely, with never a bid for revenge."

Watching them, Aeriel felt the pearlstuff subsiding, moving coolly within her, full of light. Before the kneeling prince, the grey horse shifted, danced.

"One shrug of your shoulders would have plunged me to my death," said Irrylath quietly. "Instead, faithfully, you kept your oath. Now I must keep mine. Take your vengeance, Avarclon. It is only just. I am yours. Do with me as you will."

As he fell silent, the wingèd horse tossed his head, the long horn of twisted silver glinting keen upon his brow. The air hummed softly with its passing.

"Dying in Pendar was a hard thing," the star-horse answered. "For a long time, my ghost thirsted for your death."

Coming forward, Avarclon bowed his head till his mane brushed Irrylath's cheek. His horn rested blade-sharp upon the young man's shoulder, beside the great vein of his throat. The prince neither flinched nor pulled away. He only waited.

"But all have suffered the Witch's harm," the Warhorse said, "you as much as I or any other. One thing alone will satisfy me now. Do it, and I will count our score settled and done. Help me to repeople my deserted land. Aid me in rebuilding the great kingdom over which I once kept watch. Sit upon your father's throne at Tour-of-Kings, Prince Irrylath. Be king in Avaric."

AERIEL FELT THE SWEET RUSH OF RELIEF filling her. It swept over the other listeners like a tide. Roshka and Irrylath's Istern brothers gave a ragged cheer. White-faced, the Lady Syllva leaned in the arms of her youngest, Hadin. Sabr bowed her face to one hand and set her drawn dagger back in its sheath. Irrylath himself gazed at Avarclon in astonishment. The wingèd Warhorse pulled back a pace, snorting, his breath stirring the long strands of Irrylath's black hair. The prince reached up to him.

"That I will do," he whispered, "and gladly."

He turned to Aeriel, jubilant, holding out his hand as though to share his joy with her—but Aeriel drew back. Talb's eye caught hers. Did he know? Did he guess?

"So the war is done," the duarough mage said, "and Irrylath is Avaric's king. But what of you, child? What will you do now?"

Aeriel could not reply. She wanted so to go to Irrylath, to take his hand, but she felt the radiance of the pearlstuff in her blood intensify: a warning. The Lady Syllva, her color regained, left Hadin and turned to Aeriel.

"I and my train return soon to Isternes," she said. "But most of my sons must stay behind, each to aid his lon in the rebuilding of the West. Only Hadin returns with me, for your native Pirs already has a sovereign."

The Lady held out her hand to Aeriel.

"Will you not come with us, dear child, lend Hadin and me your company? Isternes will be a lonely place without his brothers."

The Lady's eyes invited her, her smile hopeful yet sad.

"It is to my rue that I bore only sons—never a daughter to be my heir. You are my niece, the daughter of my birthsister, who once ruled my dominion in my stead. Come across the Sea-of-Dust with us," she said. "Be heir to the Ladyship of Isternes."

Aeriel shook her head, refusing the other's hand. "If it is the law in Isternes that says no man may rule as Lord, then it is an unjust law. If it is merely custom, let it be custom no more. It is Hadin who shall be with you in Isternes. Make him your heir."

Syllva and her youngestborn exchanged a glance.

"Since you wish it," the Lady replied at last, "it will be so."

Hadin bowed to Aeriel, his face full of wonder and delight. One by one, his Istern brothers came forward, each accompanying his lon. The wolf of Bern spoke first.

"Come rule in my land, which was so pleasant once. Together, we shall make it so again."

Aeriel shook her head. "Let him who was your rider rule your land."

Red Arat, one arm bandaged in a sling, came forward beside Elverlon.

"Be queen of my strange and wondrous land, Aeriel," the cockatrice urged.

Shaking her head, she answered, "Let Arat rule for me."

Dappled Zambulon came forward, Syril at his side.

"Mine is the fairest land by far," the wingèd panther purred. "I and my people would welcome you."

Again she shook her head. "Let that be Syril's task."

Brass-colored Terralon approached, accompanied by Syril's birthbrother, Lern.

"You spent your childhood in my land, great Aeriel," said the gryphon of Terrain. "Return. Be sibyl on the altar-cliffs of Orm, before whom even the satrap bows."

Sadly, Aeriel cast down her eyes. "The sibyls of Orm are no more, I fear, and your consort the sfinx has deposed the satrap for trafficking in slaves. Let Lern replace him as ruler in my stead."

Drawing near, Poratun in purple robes beckoned her from beside Ranilon.

"You have never seen my land," the wingèd

salamander said. "But it is marvelous strange and fair. Come sample it and be its queen."

Regretfully, Aeriel turned away. "Give the crown to Poratun."

Lastly, her own brother Roshka came forward beside the bronze stag Pirsalon. Hadin, who had been that lon's rider during the war, stood back holding the reins of Nightwalker, Roshka's steed. This time it was the man who spoke and not the lon.

"Erryl, my sister," said Roshka, "now called Aeriel, you are our father's firstborn and the right heir in Pirs. Return with me to take your place as suzeranee."

With the greatest sorrow yet, Aeriel shook her head. "It is true I am Pirs's rightful heir. But you have been its crown prince all the years that I was lost, a slave in Terrain. Be suzerain in my stead, brother. It is what I wish."

Roshka bowed and fell back a pace as the others had done. Another came forward, laughing, then.

"So, little pale one," Orroto-to chided, her desert walking stick in hand. Aeriel eyed the cinnamon-colored chieftess of the Ma'a-mbai and felt her spirit ever so gently lift. "You are refusing all honors and offers of crowns. Could it be, having accomplished your task, you now wish to rest?"

Wearily, Aeriel closed her eyes. If only she might rest. The dark chieftess touched her cheek.

"Come with me," she said. "Wander the dunes of Pendar as once you did. There, everyone goes where she wishes, and everyone is free."

But Aeriel could only shake her head. "Chieftess, my task is not yet done, and I am not yet free."

The other's eyes grew rueful, but at last she, too, fell back. Talb the Mage spoke.

"Daughter, I, also, must go. Now that all this water is back in the world, the mighty underland streams of Aiderlan will once more begin to flow, and someone with a small store of sorcery"—here he scoffed modestly—"should be on hand to help things along. I'd beg you to come and lend your aid, if I'd the least hope of your saying yes."

His wistfulness almost made her smile, though her heart was very sore—but a commotion parted the ranks of Syllva's bowwomen suddenly. The Isterners stepped hastily aside to allow a tight knot of little waist-high people through. None of them were any taller than Talb.

"Sorcery indeed!" the foremost snorted, her red

hair falling in four thick braids, one before, one behind each ear. "We can put all in Aiderlan to rights with machines alone, brother. You can keep your sorcery."

Maruha stood indignantly before the little mage. She was garbed all in padded leather, a round shield slung behind one shoulder and a shortsword at her belt. Aeriel spotted Collum and Brandl behind her, and others in battledress—but many in the group wore only the grey tatters of slaves. Marks upon the necks and wrists of some showed where collars and shackles had chafed, though those had now been struck away. They looked thin but flushed with triumph, still dizzy with disbelief. So these were the ones Oriencor had taken, Aeriel guessed, now rescued by their kith. Talb started back from Maruha in surprise.

"Well, sister," he exclaimed. "I vow! It has been a world's age since last we met."

"Longer, since you traipsed off to Lonwury to study your nit-pated sorcery. Never had any use for honest machinery, did you? Except apparatus for distilling your infernal drams."

She humphed in disgust. Collum and Brandl exchanged a glance which, Aeriel noted wryly, held more than a little sympathy for Talb. Maruha caught the look and glowered.

"Now your nephew has gotten like notions of running off overland to become a bard! I haven't been able to keep his fingers off that little harp since we left the City of Crystalglass."

"Nephew?" cried Talb, starting forward to embrace the younger duarough. "Young one, well met! I thought you had a family look about you. Would you be a singer of tales, a bard? Best go with the Lady Syllva then and learn her craft."

"Sooth!" exclaimed Maruha. "Such talk simply encourages him."

What more they said, Aeriel did not catch, for Irrylath, kneeling still, had reached and taken her hands. His words were low, for her alone.

"Aeriel," he whispered. "What is this, all these others holding out to you crowns and inviting you to go with them? You mean to come with me, of course."

She met his eyes. They were full of misgiving. Heavily, she shook her head. "I cannot."

His gaze grew baffled. "But the war is over," he cried. "The Witch is dead."

"And the pearl of the world's soul broken," she answered. "Ravenna's sorcery scattered to the winds. It was all that stood between us and the winding down of the world. That is the true war," she whispered, struggling. "Our victory at

Winterock has only won a respite. We must use it wisely. Someone must regather the lost soul of the world."

Irrylath's grip on her hands tightened, his words, his look suddenly desperate. "But not you. Not *you*, Aeriel! You have already done far more than enough. Let another undertake the task."

"What other?" she asked. "There is none. Ravenna chose me."

The pearlstuff in her blood stirred uneasily. *Stand firm*, it murmured. *You must not waver. Did you rescue the world only to abandon it now?*

"I must return to the City of Crystalglass," Aeriel whispered. "I must learn to read the Ancient script...."

The pearl's vision loomed before her. Overwhelmed by the task's immensity, she made to turn away. Almost roughly, the prince pulled her back to him.

"I will go with you," he started, and for a moment his eyes burned with hope.

"You cannot!" she cried. "Don't you see? You have sworn to obey the equustel's charge, to be king in Avaric...."

He stared at her, his face stricken, his breath grown short.

"Stay," Irrylath implored her. "Only stay with me, Aeriel. I will make you queen in Avaric."

Lifting her gaze, she looked past him to Sabr, dismounted now, near enough to overhear. She stood watching the two of them with astonishment and barely guarded joy.

Aeriel told Irrylath, "Avaric already has a queen."

He whirled to see to whom she looked, then turned back with a cry. "*You* are my wife. I married *you*."

Shaking her head, she touched his cheek. "Two years were all we had, love," she whispered, "and we squandered them."

The pearlstuff in her blood was seething now. *Make an end to it, quickly,* Ravenna within her warned. *If passion overrules you, all the world is lost.*

"Be king in Avaric," Aeriel managed, "and think no more of me."

Fierce triumph lit the eyes of the bandit queen. Her gaze pounced on Irrylath.

"No!" he cried. "Don't leave me. Aeriel, you are my wife, the keeper of my heart...."

Grief had her by the throat. She could not speak. The pearl's radiance within her brightened dangerously. Her breast ached where there should have been no pain. Irrylath, too, seemed to feel some twinge. He frowned, wincing, laying one hand upon his breastbone. His gaze fell on the Edge Adamantine.

"What have you done?" he gasped, astonished, like one pinned through with a sword. She knew that she must pull away from him at once, lest the roiling sorcery within her scathe him. "Aeriel, what have you done?"

"Give your heart to Sabr," she managed. "Of course you are drawn to her." Fool! she cursed herself. Fool not to have understood before. "For you see yourself in her—your very image—unbroken and unscarred. You as you might have been if the Witch had never touched you."

Sabr started eagerly forward, but her cousin warned her away with a savage look. "Never!"

Aeriel tried desperately to pull away, but he still held fiercely to her hands.

"I'll not wed Sabr."

The joy that lanced through Aeriel to hear him say it was almost too sweet to bear. She wanted to savor it, so tempted then—as she had been in the Witch's tower—to forget the world and go with him. She wanted to weep, to fall into his arms, but her eyelids were marked with white stars from the Witch's touch, and she had no power of tears anymore.

Enough. The Ancient voice reproved her sternly. *No more of this. You have sworn to renounce him for the sake of the world.*

The pearlstuff rose in a white-hot, singeing flash. Aeriel cried out in surprise, heard Irrylath's echoing cry. He dropped her hands. She saw him gazing at his own as though they were numbed or burned.

"Take care!" she cried, bitterly aware her warning came too late. She should have broken from him long since, and yet, selfishly, she had lingered. Irrylath shook his head as if dizzy. He was able to flex his fingers a little, slowly. She remembered the white fire of the burning sword and hoped fervently that his hurt was not great, not permanent. He gazed at her, dumbstruck. The chain about her wrist had begun to glow.

"The Ravenna has enchanted you," he whispered.

Aeriel tugged at the chain, but it would not come free. "Some of her sorcery is in me now."

"Has she given you her sorcery to wield at your will, or does her sorcery wield you?" he demanded, staring at the chain. "Are you now become the Ravenna's creature as wholly as I once belonged to the Witch?"

The thought horrified her. She could not answer him.

You gave your oath to me voluntarily, the pearl-stuff within reminded insistently, but Aeriel took no comfort. The fine, interlocking links of Ancient silver glimmered, unbreakably strong.

"Be my husband if you must," she bade Irrylath, "in Avaric. I shall be far away in Nu-Ravenna."

His eyes grew hard and bright, hands clenched into fists at his breast. "I'll win you back," he whispered. "On my life, I swear it! I'll find a way to break the Ancient's spell and bring you back to me."

Her heart leapt to hear him say it. But she feared he did not believe a word. How could such brave nonsense ever come to pass? Surely he must realize that Ravenna's sorcery—even scattered and diminished as it was—was far too mighty for any mortal to overcome. She had no doubt she would never see him again, and the taste was bitter, bitter on her tongue. He called her name.

"Aeriel. Aeriel!"

She could not bear the pain of gazing on him more and forced herself to turn away.

Someone was approaching over the black marsh flats, coming very slowly with a halting step. He must have been in view for some time, Aeriel realized, unnoticed by anyone. A heron, perfectly white, skimmed the air ahead of him and alighted on the ground before Aeriel.

"We missed the battle, I see," she remarked, cocking her head and looking about. "Just as well."

"Who comes?" Aeriel asked, though even as she said it, she knew. She would know his halt step anywhere. The heron fanned her crest.

"The Lighthousekeeper of Bern, of course. I was to fetch him at the proper hour. Ravenna's behest from long, long ago. We've been traveling for daymonths."

"Yes," the Lighthousekeeper panted, drawing near. "It seems an age. I feel quite spent. I was not made for such journeying. I have something for you, Lady Aeriel—for Ravenna's other daughter is, I see, no more."

He held out to her a hoop of white metal with twelve-and-one sharp, upright prongs.

"Is this what lay at the heart of your lighthouse

flame?" she asked. The pearlstuff in her blood leapt, crackling at the sight, but she herself felt no anticipation or joy.

The Keeper nodded. "My task has always been to guard it for the world's heir."

Aeriel nodded and bowed her head. He placed the circlet upon her brow. The crown felt hollow, empty. Aeriel scarcely noticed its weight. Her enchanted blood shimmered, singing and alive. The darkness was suddenly full of light. Lifting her eyes, Aeriel saw the constellation called the Maidens' Dance by some and by others the Crown wavering in heaven. Its stars drew nearer, descending, taking on the appearance of candle flames. In another moment, thirteen maidens stood about her, all made of golden light: those whose souls she had once rescued from the darkangel in Avaric. It seemed so long ago.

"Eoduin, Marrea..." She called them each by name.

"We understand at last," Marrea, the first and eldest, said, "how it was that you should come among us. We had thought you would join us in deep heaven, but we see now that it is we who must join you here below."

In the space of a moment, she dwindled, her tiny yellow flame floating in the air to alight on one of the foremost prongs of the crown, burning brilliant upon its tip. Aeriel felt a new sensation kindling within her. One by one, the other maidens followed the first. The crown felt filled now, but still feather-light. Eoduin was the last.

"Forgive me for having been so impatient to have you among us in Orm," she said. "Cold heaven has been very lonesome without you."

As she, too, assumed her place, opposite Marrea's flame, the white heron took wing and settled into the space between the two foremost prongs. Doing so, she shrank, becoming part of the crown, head bowed to her breast and her long, slender wings falling to flank the pale girl's cheeks.

Aeriel's blood answered the flame in the crown. The pearlstuff rose in her, magnified, seemed suddenly to catch fire. Aeriel felt once more a keen, far-ranging perception, very like the pearl's but immeasurably stronger. The interlocking pattern of the marsh flats unfolded before her. The stars above wheeled and circled one another like burning beads. She felt that she might see to the world's end if she tried, or even deeper into heaven.

Time enough for that, the voice of Ancient sorcery within her promised, *in NuRavenna. There, by such means, you shall regather the soul of the world. But haste now. Time is short.*

A cool, misty white fire ran along her skin. Aeriel turned back to the others standing before her. She felt utterly alone: they had all shrunk back, staring at her—the Lighthousekeeper, the Lady Syllva and the rest, even Talb—all save for Irrylath, whose head was bowed to his hands. Sabr stood by him, hands like hawks upon his shoulders. He seemed oblivious to her. Even her fierce look of victory had washed away in astonishment as she gazed at Aeriel.

It was not her eyes, though, that Aeriel sought. She found Erin among the crowd. The burning sword hung sheathed at her side, but even through the scabbard, Aeriel was aware of the blade's fire stirring and brightening, answering her own. Without hesitation, the dark girl came forward.

"And what of you, Erin?" Aeriel asked. "All have told me their intentions but you. Will you go with the Mariners among whom you were born, back to their isles in the Sea-of-Dust?"

One hand resting on the pommel of her glaive, the dark girl shook her head. "I will not. Perhaps one day. Yes, I was born among the Mariners—of that I have no doubt. But I was raised in other lands and hardly feel at ease among my own people, whose tongue I do not even speak, or among the people of Zambul that once enslaved me, or anywhere. I have had but one true friend in all my life."

For a moment, Erin cast her gaze to the sword whispering at her side, then looked up, bold.

"I care not whether some now call you Ravenna's daughter or that you have no shadow and wear a burning crown. You are the only light I know. I want no other fellowship than yours. It seems that I alone of all this throng have it in my power to choose my road. Aeriel, I would go with you."

Aeriel closed her eyes. She would not be alone then, after all. Here at the beginning, at least, one companion would accompany her.

"The Flame in Orm robbed me of my shadow," she whispered, "but I am not without one, ever. If not for you, Erin, I would be lost."

Fearlessly, the dark girl put her arms around her.

"My darkness," breathed Aeriel.

Erin answered, "My light."

Aeriel turned and faced them all.

"Fare you well," she told them. No more remained to be said.

Palms together, Syllva and her Istern sons bowed to her. Talb, Roshka, and the duaroughs made reverence. The islanders, the bowwomen, even Sabr's dismounted cavalry knelt. Orroto-to's desert folk gravely nodded. Even Pendarlon and Avarclon and the other lons saluted her. All paid homage but the king of Avaric, who wept, and the bandit queen who could not console him.

Erin still had hold of her hand. The burning crown's fire seemed to affect her no more than the fire of the sword. Aeriel was glad of it, for someone bold enough not to let her go. It would be a long road to NuRavenna. The light of the crown blazed bright against the night. As she and Erin set out, she heard Brandl's bell-sweet harp behind them, his clear, young voice raised in song:

> *"On Avaric's white plain,*
> > *where an icarus now wings*
> *To steeps of Terrain*
> > *from Tour-of-the-Kings,*
>
> *And damozels twice-seven*
> > *his brides have all become:*
> *A far cry from heaven,*
> > *a long road from home—*
>
> *Then strong-hoof of a starhorse*
> > *must hallow him unguessed*
> *If adamant's edge is to plunder*
> > *his breast.*

Then, only, may the Warhorse
   and Warrior arise
To rally the warhosts, and thunder
   the skies.

But first there must assemble
   ones icari would claim.
A bride in the temple
   must enter the flame,

With steeds found for six brothers, beyond
   a dust deepsea,
And new arrows reckoned, a wand
   given wings—

That when a princess-royal's
   to have tasted of the tree,
Then far from Esternesse's
   city, these things:

A gathering of gargoyles,
   a feasting on the stone,
The Witch of Westernesse's
   hag overthrown.

Whereafter shall commence
   such a cruel Sorceress War,
To wrest recompense
   for a land leaguered sore.

With her broadsword Bright Burning,
  the shadow Black-as-Night,
From exile returning,
  shall dare dragons' might

For love of one above who, flag unfurled,
  lone must stand,
The pearl of the soul of the world
  in her hand.

When Winterock to water
  falls flooding, foes to drown,
Ravenna's own daughter
  shall kindle the crown."

Pronunciation Guide
~

[ˈædəmənt]	adamant	ADD-uh-munt (accent first syllable)
[əˈdæməntin]	Adamantine	uh-DAMM-unn-teen (accent second syllable, *i* as in "mach*i*ne")
[ˈæriɛl]	Aeriel	AIR-ee-ell (short *a* as in "*a*rrogant")
[ˈaidərlan]	Aiderlan	EYE-dur-lann (*ai* as in "n*ai*ad," final *a*-sound midway between "l*a*nd" and "sw*a*n")
[ˈæræt]	Arat	AIR-ratt
[arl]	Arl	AHRL
[ˈarlɪʃ]	Arlish	AHR-lish
[ˈævarclɔn]	Avarclon	AV-ur-clawn (short first *a* as in "*a*venue," short *o* as in "cl*o*th")
[ˈævaʀik]	Avaric	AV-uh-rick (short first *a* as in "*a*verage," may roll *r*)
[bʌrn]	Bern	BURN
[ˈbʌrnalɔn]	Bernalon	BURN-uh-lawn

[ˈbʌrniən]	Bernean	BURN-ee-unn
[ˈbɔmba]	Bomba	BAWM-buh
[ˈbrændəl]	Brandl	BRAND-ull (two syllables, rhymes with "candle," may roll *r*)
[ˈkɔləm]	Collum	CALL-umm (short *o* as in "c*o*st")
[kɔˈrʌndəm]	corundum	core-RUN-dumm (accent second syllable)
[ˈdʌrna]	Dirna	DUR-nuh (rhymes with "Smyrna")
[daunˈwɛndiŋ]	Downwending	down-WENN-ding (accent second syllable)
[drægk]	dracg	DRA(g)CK (midway between "drag" and "rack")
[duˈarəf]	duarough	doo-AH-ruff (accent second of three syllables, several pronunciations possible, may roll *r*)
[duˈaru_x]		doo-AHR-ookh
[ˈɛlvər]	Elver	ELL-vur
[ˈɛlvɔrlon]	Elverlon	ELL-vur-lawn
[ˈɛodu ɪn]	Eoduin	EH-oh-doo-inn (major accent on first and minor accent on last of four syllables)
[ˈɛkwəstɛl]	equustel	ECK-wuss-tell (two short *e*'s)
[ˈɛrɪn]	Erin	EH-rinn
[ɛstərˈnɛssœ]	Esternesse	ess-tur-NESS-suh (accent third of four syllables)
[ˈgælnɔr]	Galnor	GAL-nor (short *a* as in "p*a*llid")
[ˈgɔləm]	golam	GOLL-umm (like "golem")
[ˈ_xadin]	Hadin	(k)HAH-deen (accent first syllable, *h* is strongly aspirate, broad *a* as in "f*a*ther," *i* as in "mach*i*ne")

[ˈɪkarɛ]	icarë	ICK-uh-reh (short *e*, as in "r*e*d")
[ˈɪkarai]	icari	ICK-uh-rye (long final *i* as in "r*i*pe")
[ˈɪkarəs]	icarus	ICK-uh-russ
[ˈɪrylaθ]	Irrylath	IH-rrew-lahth (*r* is rolled; pronounce *y* by pursing lips to say "ooh," but say "ee" instead; last syllable rhymes with "swath")
[ˈɪstərn]	Istern	ISS-turn (pronounced like "eastern," but with short *i*)
[ˈɪstərnər]	Isterner	ISS-turn-ur (pronounced like "easterner," but with short *i*)
[ɪstərˈnɛs]	Isternes	iss-tur-NESS (accent last syllable, rhymes with "sister Bess")
[lʌrn]	Lern	LURN (sounds like "learn")
[lɔn]	lon	LAWN (short *o*, as in "g*o*ne")
[ˈlɔrəlai]	lorelei	LORE-uh-lye (*ei* sounds like long *i*)
[ˈlaiən]	lyon	LYE-unn (like "lion")
[maamˈbai]	Ma'a-mbai	MAH-ahm-BYE (accent both first and last of three syllables, *ai* as in "n*ai*ad")
[mær]	Mare	MAIR (rhymes with "care")
[ˈmaRələn]	Marelon	MARR-uh-lawn (three syllables, broad *a* as in "m*a*rch")
[ˈmærɪnər]	Mariner	MAIR-inn-ur (like "mariner")
[ˈmaRea]	Marrea	MARR-ay-uh (accent first syllable, roll *r*, *e* as in "r*ei*n")
[maˈRuha]	Maruha	muh-RROO-ha (accent second syllable, roll *r*)

[ˈmɛlkior]	Melkior	MEL-kee-ore
[mir]	Mere	MEER (rhymes with "seer")
[ˈmirgɪnt]	mereguint	MEER-ghint (hard *g*, silent *u*)
[nar]	Nar	NARR
[nat]	Nat	NAHT (rhymes with "swat")
[nuRaˈvɛna]	NuRavenna	noo-ruh-VENN-uh (pronounced like "New Ravenna")
[oseˈænus]	Oceanus	oh-say-ANN-noose (two pronunciations possible)
[oₛiˈænəs]		oh-shee-ANN-uss
[ˈɔriɛŋkɔr]	Oriencor	ORE-ee-eng-core
[ɔrm]	Orm	ORM
[ɔˈrototo]	Oroto-to	ore-RROE-toe-toe (accent second syllable, roll *r*)
[ˈpɛndar]	Pendar	PENN-dar
[ˈpɛndarlɔn]	Pendarlon	PENN-dar-lawn
[pʌrs]	Pirs	PURSE
[ˈpʌrsalɔn]	Pirsalon	PURSE-uh-lawn
[ˈpʌrsiən]	Pirsean	PURSE-ee-unn (three syllables, keep *s* unvoiced, long *e* as in "seeing")
[pɔRaˈtun]	Poratun	porr-uh-TOON (roll *r* and accent last syllable, which rhymes with "moon")
[ˈRani]	Rani	RAH-nee (rhymes with "Suwannee," *r* may be rolled)
[ˈRanilɔn]	Ranilon	RAH-nih-lawn
[Raˈvɛna]	Ravenna	ruh-VENN-uh (*r* may be rolled)
[hRʊk]	rhuk	HRROOK (rhymes with "hook," *rh* is breathy and rolled)
[ˈRɔₛka]	Roshka	RROSH-kah (roll *r*)

[ˈsabʀ]	Sabr	SAH-brr (two syllables, *r* is breathy and rolled, final syllable contains no vowel sound)
[ˈskæbərd]	Scabbird	SCABB-urd (like "scabbard")
[sfɪnks]	sfinx	SFINKS (like "sphinx")
[ˈsolstar]	Solstar	SOLE-star
[ˈsolstaraiz]	Solstarrise	SOLE-star-eyes
[ˈsolstarsɛt]	Solstarset	SOLE-star-sett
[ˈsʊlva]	Syllva	SOOLL-vah (first syllable rhymes with "pull," broad *a* as in "w*a*nder")
[ˈsyrœl]	Syril	SEWE-rull (pronounce *y* by pursing lips to say "ooh," but say "ee" instead)
[talb]	Talb	TAHLB (*a*-sound midway between "sh*a*ll" and "w*a*llow")
[ˈtælɪs]	Talis	TAL-iss (short *a* as in "p*a*lace")
[tɛˈren]	Terrain	teh-REIGN (like "terrain")
[tɛˈrenian]	Terrainean	teh-REIGN-ee-unn (as in "sub*terranean*")
[ˈvæmpair]	vampyre	VAMM-pire (like "vampire")
[wɛstərˈnɛssœ]	Westernesse	west-ur-NESS-suh (accent third of four syllables)
[ˈwɛstrən]	Westron	WEST-runn (rhymes with "BEST-run")
[ˈwɪntərɔk]	Winterock	WINN-tur-ock (like "winter rock")
[ˈzæmbul]	Zambul	ZAMM-bool (short *a* as in "*a*mber," last syllable rhymes with "cool")
[ˈzæmbulən]	Zambulan	ZAAM-boo-lunn
[ˈzæmbulɔn]	Zambulon	ZAMM-boo-lawn (short first *a* as in "*a*mple," short *o* as in "*o*n")

Let your imagination fly with the best in fantasy

MAGIC CARPET

BOOKS

The Kingdom of Kevin Malone   (0-15-201191-9) $6.00
BY SUZY MCKEE CHARNAS
Amy finds a magical world in Central Park where bully Kevin Malone is a hero.
Worse still, he needs Amy to save his kingdom and himself. Will she help this
punk she doesn't even like?

Knight's Wyrd   (0-15-201520-5) $6.00
BY DEBRA DOYLE AND JAMES D. MACDONALD
Will Oddosson is told his wyrd—his fate—on the eve of his knighting: He will
meet Death before a year has passed. Soon he is beset by one evil beast after
another. Which will be his wyrd?

DIANE DUANE's thrilling wizardry series

So You Want to Be a Wizard   (0-15-201239-7) $6.50
Fleeing a bully, Nita discovers a manual on wizardry in her library. But magic
doesn't solve her problems—in fact, they've only just begun!

Deep Wizardry   (0-15-201240-0) $6.00
The novice wizards join a group of dolphins, whales, and one giant shark in an
ancient magical ritual—a ritual that must end with a bloody sacrifice.

High Wizardry   (0-15-201241-9) $6.00
Nita and Kit face their most terrifying challenge yet: Nita's bratty little sister,
Dairine—the newest wizard in the neighborhood!

A Wizard Abroad   (0-15-201207-9) $6.00
Nita's Irish vacation from magic turns out to be the opposite! Ireland is even more
steeped in wizardly dangers than the States. So much for a vacation abroad. . . .

Magic Carpet Books is a registered trademark of Harcourt Brace & Company.

ALAN GARNER's classic Alderley tales

The Weirdstone of Brisingamen (0-15-201766-6) $6.00
All of Evil's minions are working to stop Colin and Susan from returning the
Weirdstone to its rightful owner, the wizard Cadellin, but the earth's fate
depends on them.

The Moon of Gomrath (0-15-201796-8) $6.00
Colin and Susan's bonfire does more than warm the night—it calls forth the
Wild Hunt and launches a final desperate struggle between the children and the
forces of darkness.

Elidor (0-15-201797-6) $6.00
BY ALAN GARNER
When the four Watson children stumble into Elidor, a world one step removed
from our own, they begin a frightening adventure that stretches their courage to
the limit. Yet far scarier is what happens when they return home. . . .

Two fantasy classics by MOLLIE HUNTER

The Smartest Man in Ireland (0-15-200993-0) $5.00
To prove his boast of being the smartest man in the land, Patrick Kentigern
Keenan tries to outwit the fairies. But wit is not much against an opponent who
has magic. . . .

The Walking Stones (0-15-200995-7) $5.00
A wise old man gives Donald the knowledge—and the power—to prevent
developers from destroying an ancient mystical circle of stones.

A Dark Horn Blowing (0-15-201201-X) $6.00
BY DAHLOV IPCAR
Nora is stolen away one night and taken to Erland. There she must tend sickly
Prince Elver and avoid the eye of his father, the wicked Erl King, who would
have Nora for a wife.

The Forgotten Beasts of Eld (0-15-200869-1) $6.00
BY PATRICIA A. McKILLIP
Sybel's only family is the group of animals that live on Eld Mountain. She cares
nothing for humans until she is given a child to raise, changing her life utterly.

Tomorrow's Wizard (0-15-201276-1) $6.00
BY PATRICIA MacLACHLAN
What's wrong with Tomorrow's apprentice? Can he not hear the High Wizard's
warnings? Or is it that the apprentice would rather be a human instead of a
wizard?

Are All the Giants Dead? (0-15-201523-X) $7.00
BY MARY NORTON
To stop Dulcibel from marrying a toad, James must get Jack-of-the-Beanstalk and Jack-the-Giant-Killer to leave retirement and to kill the last of the giants.

The first book in EDITH PATTOU's epic Songs of Eirren

Hero's Song (0-15-201636-8) $6.00
The trail of his sister's kidnappers leads Collun to a giant white wurme whose slime is acid to the touch, a wurme that Collun must kill if he is to rescue his sister and save his world.

MEREDITH ANN PIERCE's classic Darkangel Trilogy

The Darkangel (0-15-201768-2) $6.00
Aeriel must kill the wicked Darkangel before he finds his fourteenth bride—even though within him is a spark of goodness that could redeem even *his* evil.

A Gathering of Gargoyles (0-15-201801-8) $6.00
Saving the darkangel Irrylath was only the beginning. Now Aeriel must confront his mother, the dread White Witch—and her bloodthirsty vampyre sons. . . .

The Pearl of the Soul of the World (0-15-201800-X) $6.00
The stunning conclusion to the trilogy finds Aeriel at a dangerous juncture. Irrylath has been captured and the Witch seems sure of victory—unless Aeriel can solve the Riddle of Ravenna and unlock the magic of an iridescent pearl.

River Rats (0-15-201411-X) $6.00
BY CAROLINE STEVERMER
After a nuclear war, a group of teens steer a riverboat up and down the Mississippi, playing rock and roll concerts and fleeing the adults who wrecked the world in the first place.

Laughs and wonder from master wit VIVIAN VANDE VELDE

A Hidden Magic (0-15-201200-1) $5.00
Plain Princess Jennifer must rescue the vain—and cursed—prince from his own stupidity, as well as a lisping dragon, a dim-witted giant, and a cast of crazies in this witty fractured fairy tale

A Well-Timed Enchantment (0-15-201765-8) $6.00
Deanna drops her watch into a well and is magicked away to eighth-century France, where her watch, if it falls into the wrong hands, will change the world. She must find it first!

JANE YOLEN's classic Pit Dragon Trilogy

Dragon's Blood   (0-15-200866-7) $6.00
Jakkin's only hope for freedom is to kidnap and train a dragon of his own, a
dragon that will grow into a champion in the vicious fighting pits of Austar IV.

Heart's Blood   (0-15-200865-9) $6.00
When his beloved vanishes, Jakkin and his dragon, Heart's Blood, become
embroiled in a plot deadlier than any dragon pit match.

A Sending of Dragons   (0-15-200864-0) $6.00
On the run from government forces, Jakkin and Akki stumble upon a twisted
sect of dragon worshipers.

The Transfigured Hart   (0-15-201195-1) $5.00
BY JANE YOLEN
Is Richard crazy? Or is there a unicorn hiding in the Five Mile Wood? And how
will Richard and Heather protect the unicorn from the hunters who don't
recognize its beauty?

Wizard's Hall   (0-15-202085-3) $6.00
BY JANE YOLEN
Poor Thornmallow. The only talent he has is for making messes of the simplest
spells. But when Wizard's Hall is threatened by a fearsome beast, it is
Thornmallow—using his one talent—who saves the school.

Ask for Magic Carpet Books at your local bookstore.
To order directly, call 1-800-543-1918.
Major credit cards accepted.

Let your imagination fly

... by joining the Magic Carpet Book Club!

Buy any three Magic Carpet books, and get a free fantasy novel!

Getting your free fantasy novel is easy. Just buy three Magic Carpet books and clip the proof of purchase tab from the corner of each book club page. (If the Magic Carpet books you buy do not have a book club page, send in your register receipts listing each title purchased as proof of purchase.) Then fill out the order form below and send it, along with proof of all three purchases, to:

Magic Carpet Book Club
Harcourt Brace & Company
525 B Street, Suite 1900
San Diego, CA 92101

And we'll send you a free book!

(please print)

Name: _____ Age: _____

Street Address: _____

City: _____ State: ____ Zip: _____

Favorite Book: _____

Send to: MAGIC CARPET BOOK CLUB
            Harcourt Brace & Company
            525 B Street, Suite 1900
            San Diego, CA 92101

Reproductions or copies of proof of purchase tabs (or receipts) will not be accepted and will receive no response. Harcourt Brace will choose which titles will be sent as premiums, depending on availability. Premiums will be shipped within 4–8 weeks of receipt of order form. Harcourt Brace is not responsible for lost or incomplete orders and may discontinue the book club at any time. Offer expires two years after date on proof of purchase.

Magic Carpet Books is a registered trademark of Harcourt Brace & Company.

5/99

The Pearl of the Soul of the World

0-15-201800-X

PROOF OF PURCHASE